THE READING

THE Reading

Barbara Monier

Altitude
Cover art by Sandra Dawson
sandradawson.net

First Edition   ISBN 13: 978-1-956872-60-6

AMIKA PRESS
466 Central AVE #23 Northfield IL 60093   847 920 8084
info@amikapress.com   Available for purchase on amikapress.com

Edited by John K. Manos. Designed and typeset by Sarah Koz. Body in Minion Pro, designed by Robert Slimbach in 1990. Titles in Didot, designed by Firmin Didot in 1783 and Adrian Frutiger, for Linotype, in 1992. Thanks to Nathan Matteson.

The inspiration for this novel came from two sources:

J.D. Salinger, who wrote the short story
"For Esmé—with Love and Squalor"

And JTS, who wrote a letter

"Nobody's aiming to please, here.
More, really, to edify, to instruct."

—J.D. Salinger
"For Esmé—with Love and Squalor"

INTRODUCTION

IN THE LATE WINTER OF 1955, MOM SAT IN ONE OF THE BUR-
gundy fake-leather chairs in Dr. McClelland's waiting room,
leafing through an issue of *The New Yorker* from 1950. The
décor was in keeping with the magazine's vintage—the steel-
frame chairs, as well as the muted peach walls and the tall
metal rack where she had chosen the magazine, had been exactly the same since my mother's childhood—a room separate from the passing of time. Ankles crossed primly but dis-
tracted by the lethargic, lightheaded way she had been feeling
for days, my mother glanced briefly out the sole window at
the dismal sky, searching for signs of an early spring. When
she glanced back down, she was too fuzzy-brained to be de-
voting any serious attention to the magazine's contents. But a
particular illustration caught her eye amid the flick of pages.

My mother often mused about the seemingly haphazard
chain of events. That she would pick up a magazine she generally looked down on for its stuffy snobbery. That she would
leaf through the pages in her absent-minded lassitude and
somehow be captivated by a small illustration of a flower
market at the bottom of two solid pages of type. That the unobtrusive, restrained typeface of the story that filled those

two pages would catch her eye. "For Esmé—with Love and Squalor." She glanced at the writer's name. My mother had not heard of J.D. Salinger, though she considered herself a very serious reader. She glanced back at the title. And she swore that in that exact moment, staring at the title for the second time, she understood the reason for her malaise. She was, she felt certain, pregnant. She further understood, beyond a shadow of a doubt, that her quickly-dividing embryo was to be a girl, and that the girl's name might be Esmé—depending on whether she liked the story as much as her intuition told her she would.

Does our parents' choice of name influence who we are to become?

Swahili speakers in Kenya give their babies a name at birth, which usually refers to the newborn's appearance or the circumstances surrounding the birth itself. But up to forty days afterward, the parents and paternal grandparents choose the final, adult name with great care.

In parts of India, it is believed that each child's birth is ruled by a *nakshatra,* or birth star constellation. The nakshatra is thought to play a significant role in determining the characteristics of the child, and many parents follow certain sounds or syllables based on the nakshatras—all of which are determined after the child is born.

Some parents in China seek fortune tellers to help name their children instead of relying on more usual traditions. Some believe that the child may lack one of the four elements, depending on the time and circumstances of the birth, which can lead parents to choose a name that incorporates the element the child could be deficient in.

Dr. McClelland's nurse Ruth opened the inner waiting room door to usher my mother into the doctor's office. My mother had known Ruth since Ruth had been the nurse for the first Dr. McClelland, when Ruth was a young woman and my mother was a little girl. Ruth's face looked remarkably similar to how she had always looked, but her body had undergone a gradual widening that gave the impression that her younger self had been somehow inflated, as if Ruth's body had expanded in direct proportion to her diminishing time.

"Ruth," my mother said, waving the April 8, 1950 issue of *The New Yorker* back and forth. "I know why I've been feeling so poorly. I'm going to have a baby!"

Ruth well understood that she was getting on in years and feared that she didn't always catch on to things as she once had. "The magazine told you that you're pregnant?"

My mother laughed and put her hand gently on Ruth's arm. "No, no. I just figured it out while I was *reading* the magazine. And she's going to be a girl. I'm sure of it."

Ruth dabbed at her eye and said, "Thank the Lord, that I have lived long enough to see my babies have babies of their own," and she threw her arms around my mother and drew her as close as Ruth's tremendous bosom would allow. "If only Dr. McClelland could have lived to see this. The first Dr. McClelland."

"I don't need to see the doctor, Ruth. Not yet. Not so early. But would you please ask Dr. McClelland if I can borrow this magazine? There's something I'd like to read. I promise to return it."

"I don't need to ask him, and you don't need to return it. For heaven's sake, do you think Dr. McClelland has any idea what's in his own waiting room? Just get your rest, and make sure that sweet boy takes good care of you. You can tell him I said so." It is highly likely that Ruth—who had known my father, like my mother, since his birth—was the only person who ever thought of him as a "sweet boy." Not that he didn't have a deep warmth and a certain sweetness, but it was so overshadowed by his towering, smoldering seriousness. Even when I was a young child, even when he laughed and played with me, I always sensed a weight. It was as if gravity exerted a stronger pull on him, and he could never break free.

"I don't think two people could have been happier than we have been."

It was not until many years later that I realized my father had stolen that line from Virginia Woolf's suicide note to her husband.

"Never, never blame your mother, Esmé," my father had written. "I don't think two people could have been happier than we have been."

I could not read when I was five years old. I had not been to school yet and so still lived in a world of runes and hieroglyphics that remained one of many mysterious parts that comprised the realm of older people. I could not understand what my daddy had been thinking when I found the envelope underneath my pillow. I found it when I reached for my pajamas, which I folded up each morning and placed under my pillow to wear again that night. I knew his handwriting, and I could read my own name—E S M E—which he had written in large blue letters with rounded, curly edges.

On the other side of the envelope, there were more letters written across the flap: "S-E-C-R-E-T."

I put the envelope back where I'd found it.

When my mother came in to read a story and kiss me goodnight, I asked her what S-E-C-R-E-T spelled. She told me, and I decided that I needed to find a very special, very s-e-c-r-e-t place to hide the envelope the next morning. "Can you read me two stories tonight? I'm a little wee bit scared."

Two stories?" my mother said. "Goodness! I suppose if they're short ones, we can. Just tonight, though."

"When is Daddy going to be home?" I asked her.

"I'm not sure," my mother said. "I'm never sure. But you know he always checks on you. Whenever he gets home."

"Promise?" I asked.

"Of course, I promise, silly billy" she said. "He always does."

FALL 2019

CHAPTER 1

I HAVE BEEN READING MY BOOKS ALOUD TO AUDIENCES, AND signing copies, and shaking hands, and making small talk, for most of my life. I have never been able to figure out why I get *so* nervous sometimes—jumpy and clammy and hands shaking—and other times, not nervous at all. At those times, I feel comfy and relaxed, like every single person staring at me is a kind and kindred soul who wishes me nothing but the best. But this was one of the nervous times.

Sometimes I wonder if my past catches up with me in a funny sort of way. I think about where I came from, the distance I've traveled in life, and the distance feels so far that I need to remind myself that it's real.

I came from a place where dreams were small. Not small because folks lacked the courage, or the vision, to dream bigger, but because small dreams were a great pleasure, a gentle way to approach a life of contentment. The people directly across the street from Mom and me lived in a tiny little house. I had no brothers or sisters, and no father from the time I was five. I watched the Kimballs' comings and goings from our windows. They were my model of everything a family was supposed to be. As a family of five, they crawled all over one another just going about the business of living their lives in their little home. They made giant bowls of popcorn and watched TV together. They whipped up batches of frosting for no special reason and made them into sandwiches with graham crackers. They had loud arguments. They laughed all the time. The two older children were already teenagers when the family was able to afford their first dishwasher. They rang our doorbell to tell us the news. They invited Mom and me over to see it, and they offered us frosting sandwiches. They—the Kimball family—walked on air, such was the level of their glee.

Before that reading, I found myself thinking about the Kimball family, smiling at the thought of their graham crackers bookending a thick slab of pink frosting.

Perhaps it's not the past that catches up with me, but rather the other way around. Perhaps I get so lost in the past that it's the present that takes me by surprise.

I parked right in front of the old Irish pub where the reading was scheduled. I had gotten there plenty early. I always got to the reading locations early. I would check out the room, feel the feel of it for a while. Rooms hold their histories, their stories, if you take the time to pay attention, look around, and listen to the walls. Some rooms hold on to their stories; these rooms are grim and tight-fisted and fearful that their tales, their precious histories, will be stolen from them, and they will be left with nothing. Other rooms are dying to tell you about their pasts. It leaks out everywhere—the place where broken paneling reveals the tattered stuffing within the walls where a chair toppled during a drunken argument. The chip on a faded picture frame of an equally faded painting holds the memory of an exuberant toast given during a bachelorette party, though the marriage was fraught with deception from well before the wedding itself. The exact places where much-varnished wood has been rubbed raw by a bartender who polishes endlessly when conversations sadden him past the point of endurance. He sidles along the bar, moving away from the words. He rubs, and he rubs.

This was a friendly room. Old, even tired, but welcoming. A room that stretched out its hand and let you know it was pleased that you had come.

Nonetheless, I was nervous before that reading. I ordered a glass of red wine from the server and was thrilled that it was such a generous pour. Clutching my wine tankard as if it were a lifeline, I sat down at a table near the far back of the lengthy, narrow-ish room to look over the passage I would be reading. Except what I had thought was the far back of the room turned out to the far *front,* which became clear when a woman began setting up the microphone right next to where I sat. The woman was very tall, with a wild head of hair that crowned a broad body. She was one of those people who managed to project a strong air of dramatic exuberance well before they opened their mouths and said a word. It might have been the vintage mini skirt and thigh-high boots rather than an astute acuity on my part that gave her away, plus the fact that she took a breathtaking amount of time to set a simple microphone stand in the center of the room and rest the microphone in the stand's holder.

I supposed that I was sitting a few short feet away from where I would be standing when I read from my most recent book. That's why I was there, in this room, trying to settle into the accumulation of what had occurred in all the time before I was due to stand in front of that microphone, which was still in the future as I was thinking all of this.

I reminded myself to attend to the details of the evening with particular care because Gino wasn't able to come, and I would want to tell him all about it. The more detail the better, in fact, because the reading would provide a topic of conversation other than Gino's recent suggestion that I move in with him.

Ah, yes, there was that. I acknowledged the double whammy that undoubtedly contributed to my jitters that evening. Number one: that Gino, my boyfriend, if such a term can even be used at my age, had dropped the *bomb*. Right on my vintage dining room table in my tasteful vintage apartment, right in the middle of dinner, right between bites of gnocchi with three-mushroom sauce that I had made from scratch. Number two: that after dropping the bomb, he wasn't able to come to the reading. I was relieved for the time alone—away from him—and, also, I was furious about his absence.

The tradition of this particular reading series had historically been to honor the guest author with a long string of Mardi Gras beads—not the plain ones with uniform round beads, but rather the necklaces that sported various large plastic butterflies and *fleurs de lis* and other delightfully trashy trinkets. When the broad woman in the miniskirt finished making minute microphone adjustments for me, she introduced me while draping the necklace around my neck. I thanked the assembled audience and told them that I felt festooned by the beads. Festooned. A truly wonderful word. The instant that my lips rounded to produce the "oo" sound, I relaxed completely.

Once I donned my reading glasses—just after finishing the sentence and savoring the word "festooned" —the people sitting around their small tables went out of focus, a blurred sea of general outlines and small movements. My glasses drew the words on the pages I read into precise clarity, the letters so sharp it pulled me into the page, as if I had become an ant or a gnat walking among gigantic configurations of lines and loops and dots.

Long ago I learned how to look up from my book at regular intervals without losing my place during readings. I learned how to point my eyes in the general direction of an individual audience member's eyes when I did this, though the face was a disorienting muddle. I disappeared completely into the words, my own world of words and their sounds and their meaning and the story they told.

Removing my glasses at the end of a reading was like coming up for air after being under water, holding my breath for as long as I could, seeing and hearing the world above the water re-emerge all at once. The sea of general shapes and small movements transformed into real people. Faces smiled at me.

A young couple who had been sitting in the front row leapt up to shake my hand with great fervor and tell me that both of them were planning to buy the book.

I made my way down the central aisle of the room amid outstretched hands and thank you's and a general murmur of comments. A tall, gray-haired man toward the back of the room stood up when I was still twenty paces away, smiling a wide smile and looking expectant. After various audience members had spoken to me, I glanced in his direction before I went through the doorway to the adjoining room where I would sign books.

Although there was a clear path between him and me, he walked the distance slowly, as if making his way through a dense crowd or across difficult terrain. "Hi," he said.

I smiled and said hello.

"Do you have any idea who I am?" he asked me. "Do you recognize me?"

I didn't recognize him, and immediately felt embarrassed, suddenly thrust into one of those recurring dreams where you have forgotten to attend a class for an entire semester and you find yourself sitting at a desk with the final exam staring up at you. "I'm so sorry," I said. "I'm afraid I don't…"

"It's Tom Killarney," he said.

I gasped.

I threw both arms around him.

CHAPTER 2

I HATED THAT SCHOOL. THAT HATED SCHOOL IN THAT DREADful town. That dreadful town in the part of the world where winter was not even winter. Not the light snowfalls that dusted each twig of each tree and lay spread out across the hills of Clarion, Pennsylvania, where I had grown up. Where the tiny footprints of birds and chipmunks and squirrels left their perfect imprints across our yards. In this feckless land, winter was nothing more than an endless gray sky that spit intervals of sleet. The sleet froze on the ground, making the school an ugly and hazardous wasteland of ice. A wasteland that betrayed us and made us fall down and spit on us as we lay on the ground.

A year so bad that I passed the time mainly by drinking too much, though I had arrived at the school a novice drinker. A year so bad that I got an ungodly amount of pleasure from barfing out the window of my fourth-floor dormitory room. I didn't plan this and was likely too far gone in my misery to have thought of such a magnificent metaphor. I had choked down most of a bottle of Southern Comfort and was, quite simply, too drunk to make it to the bathroom. Being that drunk also meant, as it turned out, that I could not lean my head very far out of the beautiful Gothic window without losing my balance. I held on to each side of the window frame to steady myself and leaned my chin on the sill. Hence, the vomit cascaded down the entire length of the side wall, where the winter temperatures froze it in place. And where it remained for a very long time. A slight warming of the temperature, or a sleety mix, would cause sections of the whole to trickle down, creeping its way through the brick and ivy as the mass oozed farther down the wall. Sometimes, a larger chunk would break off all at once and hit the ground below.

I checked my vomit every day, as if it were a pet, as if it were something precious whose care was my honor and responsibility. By early spring, the last vestiges of the only Southern Comfort I would ever drink were gone, and I had decided I would not be returning to the dreaded school the following year.

I wanted to leave so much that I had begun counting down the days, making large X's on an enormous wall calendar like a child marking the time until Christmas, or the end of a school year with a teacher whose dislike of teaching was only surpassed by their hated of children.

It seemed the day would never come, that I would remain stuck in the purgatory of this hated school in this dreaded town forever. But at last, there remained only one date on the calendar that did not have an X through it.

The year had wound down to my last night on campus. All I wanted to do was say goodbye. Goodbye, goodbye, goodbye, goodbye. It was time; it was finally time. I had nothing left to do but take my victory lap around the campus and hug

hug kiss kiss the assorted souls who had weathered the winter of my discontent alongside me. I was gleeful. I was drunk, as usual. I was pressed for time.

I could not find my friend Tommy. Rob hadn't seen him. Pauly hadn't seen him. Brent had seen him earlier, but…. Charlie said, yeah, he was just here. I'm pretty sure he's in the bathroom, Charlie said. As I mentioned, I was drunk. And pressed for time. I flung open the door to the men's bathroom on the floor of his dormitory, and found Tommy unzipped and just beginning to eject an impressively forceful stream from what seemed to me, having little to no experience here, to also be a remarkable distance from the target.

Tommy turned his head when he heard my voice, and I began the delivery of my goodbye message. Then the overall nature of the situation seemed to occur to him, as he registered —in rapid succession—shock, surprise, perplexity, amusement, and all-out mirth, as evidenced by an open-mouthed belly laugh. My own emotions, amazingly enough, ran much the same gamut, but in reverse, as Tommy had continued to pee an enormous, unwavering stream the entire time that I had been talking and he had been laughing.

I was amazed and—in my drunken state—felt like it was one of the most interesting and significant and noteworthy things that had happened to me in that entire year. I remarked on this to Tommy. A small crowd had gathered in the men's bathroom, as word passed about the location of my farewell; so there was, in fact, a group of people watching me watching Tommy Killarney pee while I said my last goodbye. He zipped up and we hugged and I practically skipped back to my room knowing I would leave this entire world behind me the next morning.

I did not see Tommy Killarney again.

How could I have imagined that forty-two years later, the man I hugged in a urinal would come to my reading and tell me that I had changed the course of his life?

CHAPTER 3

ON THE DAY AFTER THE NIGHT BEFORE, I SAT AT MY WRIT-ing desk with my laptop open but untouched in front of me. I drank my scrumptious fresh coffee from my favorite mug, gave my beloved old dog an occasional pat, and I pondered. I awakened early, as has long been my wont, regardless of what the previous night may have looked like, and I engaged in my assortment of other deeply entrenched habits. There are quite a number of them, and I am wholly attached to each and every one.

My writing desk had been custom-made for me from old barn wood that I had stained to a rich reddish brown. The top was unsanded and irregular. Nail holes and gouges riddled the surface; some went all the way through and showed glimpses of the floor below. It was roughhewn and rustic and very difficult to picture in the glass-and-steel castle in the sky where Gino lived, where he had asked me to live. Last evening, in fact, sitting at the authentic Shaker dining room table that was less than five feet from where I sat at my writing desk. Last evening when he unmoored me with his request to shack up, a mere couple of hours before the reading where Tommy Killarney emerged from the mists of the distant past.

One man proposing a future. Another man brokering the past.

I sipped my coffee, and I listened for the cardinal's distinctive song, as I did every morning.

On the mornings that I heard the jubilant bird, I ran to the window and scanned the trees in search of his brilliant red body. I would then search for his mate, knowing that cardinal pairs stay close to one another at all times. Deeply bonded, cardinals are. It moved me profoundly, until I remembered that they are, in fact, birds. Incapable of thought. Devoid of emotion. Their behavior forever bound up in instinct and biological determinants that were utterly beyond their consciousness. Search as I might, I had to conclude that my beloved cardinals had nothing valuable to offer me about my own future with Gino.

I listened for the people on the stairs, as I also did each morning.

The one from the basement started it. He crawled up from his underground lair, from the smell of epoxy that he used for his projects, from the array of fluorescent vests that he wore to work. He took up residence on the front stairs of the four-unit apartment building where I had lived for the past twenty-five years.

Early in the morning, he was on the stairs. Late into the night, still on the stairs.

Others began to gather. I never knew where they came from. There would just be another voice, a conversation, coming from the stairs. Or I would come home and have to step around and between others, bodies leaning this way and that as I made my way through their habitat. They did not seem to be of any common stripe or ilk, rather an assortment of types seemingly bound only by the proximity of their living situations. They amounted to their own depiction of "give me your tired, your poor…" Former frat boys with close shaves and precise parts in their short hair, and artfully disheveled high school dropouts who picked through trash for found treasure they would use in their art, and tatted up intellectuals with one pant leg perennially rolled up for their ride to work where they painstakingly experimented with combinations whose end result was a standout new cocktail—all stood shoulder-to-shoulder. All of them were many years younger than I—decades, more likely.

Writers eavesdrop. We nurture the lifelong habit of it, reveling in the possibility of inspiration, mentally rubbing our hands together in glee when presented with a tidbit that we can steal outright and cast as our own. But these people were my neighbors. I didn't want to hear them, tried to *not* hear them, but they were *on the stairs,* and I was on the first floor. There was really no escape.

Sometimes I would take a long walk go for coffee invent an errand visit a friend drive to the lakefront, all with the hope that when I returned, the stairs would be an open space—no residents. No clutter and detritus of citizens who had created their own fiefdom, on my stairs.

In the evenings, the sound of the stair dwellers would swell like great ocean waves. Still, occasional single voices would ring out like a carillon bell, random snippets that made no sense and created ripples of unsettledness within me: "…had to escape my marriage under the cover of darkness…" "…heard you can't ever get rid of that smell, no matter what you do…" "No, no, *that* wasn't the time I got shot; that was…"

I sighed a great sigh, for I knew that I would miss the stairway people terribly, painfully, should I move to Gino's. I admitted to myself that I sometimes took that walk or ran that errand just to have an excuse to exchange a few words with them. To pick my way up the stairs and drink in their lolling, sprawling youth, the bonds of their disparate fraternity.

CHAPTER 4

WHEN I HAD FINISHED MY POT OF COFFEE, PONDERED THE cardinals and grown preemptively nostalgic for the people on the stairs, I reached for my phone. "Pippa," I said into my cell, "how would you describe my relationship with Liam?"

There was a pause of noteworthy length before Pippa said, "Esmé, are you all right? Have you been up all night writing? Swear to me that you haven't been drinking at this hour of the morning."

"What?" I said, "No! How can you ask such a thing? No!"

"Don't act like I'm the one who's seeming crazy here. You don't even say hello; then you ask me about Liam and you. A question you've never asked me before. Not in all this time."

"Well…" was all I could think to say.

"Jesus, it's been, what? More than thirty years since he died?" Pippa said.

"Oh, well, yes," was all I could think to say.

"So, take that as a question," Pippa said. "After all this time? Why are you asking this now?"

"Gino asked me to move in with him," I said. "Last night."

"Ah," she said. "Well, you do sound a little like someone just murdered your dog. I guess that explains it." Pippa always did find me utterly transparent. No secrets from that one.

"I don't think I sound *that* bad," I said. "It's just…a bit hard to wrap my head around. Oĸ, *very* hard to wrap my head around."

Pippa made some indecipherable snort or grunt without really furthering the conversation.

"I did mean it as a serious question, Pip," I said. "What were we like? Liam and me?"

"Yes. Serious question," she said. "Sorry, sweetie. Sorry. It's just that…you woke me up…with a pretty…unexpected question."

"I really have no idea how we appeared to other people," I said. "Never thought about it much until just now. And just now, it seems important. I don't know why. But it does. So, I'm asking."

There was another pause, and following a deep, audible breath, Pippa came back with her serious voice. "Geez, Esmé. I mean, geez. You guys were intense. *So* intense. It was hard to be in a room with the two of you, to tell you the truth. You were *so* wrapped up in each other. It was great, kind of, and it was *weird*. It was like…you had crawled inside one another's bodies or something. Or souls. More like you'd crawled into each other's souls." As Pippa sighed again, I was aware of how much I *loved* what she was describing. "Like I said," she continued. "Great. Weird. Both."

It was my turn to make a non-descript audible sound. I felt myself leaning forward in my chair, leaning into her words as if I could draw closer to the person I had been. I wanted to hear more about the earlier version of me.

"I know what you're thinking, Esmé. You're thinking that doesn't sound a whole lot like you and Gino."

"I wasn't, actually," I said.

"You will. I know you. Just remember. Your relationship with Liam had its pluses, but it had its minuses, too."

"So you said…"

"For one thing, just for starters, it was that relentless intensity of Liam's that led him to wander off on his own personal Vision Quest and end up splattered on the side of a desert highway."

"'Splattered? Did you just say 'splattered' on the side of a highway? Jesus!"

"I'm sorry. I don't mean to be harsh. Sorry." Pippa's voice always got a tiny bit whiny when she was revved up and trying to make a point. "I loved Liam. I knew him before you did, remember?"

"Of course, I remember," I said.

"He died so long ago. So long. Long enough for you to write books and build a career and live so much life. Alone. All of it. Alone. Wouldn't it be…kind of great to have some company…for the home stretch?"

"Company," I said.

"Yes, company. Seriously, it's hard for me to imagine being in a room with Liam at this point. That was a whole different time in our lives. That fever-pitch energy of his makes me want to take a nap just thinking about it."

"A nap," I said. It was a lifelong habit of mine that when I could not think of anything else to say, I repeated what the other person had said. It drove me crazy that I did this, but I supposed it was better to buy some time to think rather than spout something inane.

"You stopped writing poetry because of Liam, because Liam needed to be the poet—the only poet—in the relationship," Pippa said.

"I was a terrible poet," I said. "The world rejoiced when I stopped writing poetry."

"So you say, but that's not why you stopped. Not really." Pippa said nothing for a time, and neither did I. She added, "He took up most of the air in any room he was in, dazzling though he could be. Gino shares the air."

We let ourselves sit in silence for a while, a comfortable silence this time, borne of the gift of long friendship.

"Maybe you should try therapy," Pippa ventured. "Maybe it would help to have someone who could talk this through with you. You know, focused specifically on the…issues here."

"Ha!" I said. "Ha ha. Need I remind you of how it went the last time you suggested therapy to me?"

When Liam got splattered on the side of a desert highway, as Pippa had so grotesquely worded it, I existed at the bottom of a very deep and very dark pit for a long, long time. Everything and everyone lurked as distant shadows—warbly, and lacking color, and without substance—like being at the bottom of a swimming pool and watching cardboard cartoon characters peering into the water.

Pippa took me by the hand in so many different ways during that awful time, one of which had been to find a therapist for me, book an appointment, and drive me there. Pippa and I sat in her parked car in front of the therapist's tidy, modest house. Pip made a valiant attempt to buoy me with a promise of coffee and pastry afterward, and she squeezed my hand. When I opened the car door and dutifully scooted out, Pippa leaned over and said, "Her name is Anne. Did I tell you?"

"Anne. Just like my mom," I said. "I love her already."

Pippa heaved one of the amplified sighs I knew so well and said, "Give it a chance. Just talk."

"Do I just…what?…knock on the front door?" As if responding to a cue, the front door opened right then, and an exceptionally tall, exceptionally slender older woman offered a practiced and professional smile, exactly midway between a blank face and a wide grin, completely open to interpretation. I thought she looked like a Picasso painting, perhaps because her chic haircut and tasteful jewelry presented such a dramatic contrast to her graceless old lady outfit and orthopedic shoes that the overall effect was of someone out of whack in the same distorted way.

"Esmé, welcome, I'm Anne," she extended her arm to the side, a gesture meant to usher me inside.

I turned my head and gave Pippa a final, pleading look.

"Promise me that you'll be a nice person. Don't terrify her." Pippa made a perky thumbs-up gesture then gave an exaggerated wave. She pulled away from the curb quite slowly. I think she was half expecting that I might make a mad dash and chase her car.

Instead, I offered a limp smile to Anne as a friendly gesture, but I continued to stand at the curb. I had no idea what the protocol might be for exchanging words before we were inside and seated. I needed the slight bit of extra time the steps between the curb and Anne's front door would yield me. I was not quite ready to have my every word and gesture dissected and scrutinized just yet. More importantly, I was not disposed to lay down any cards that remained clutched to my chest, exactly where I wanted them to be.

I screwed up the small reserve of courage I had and walked to Anne's front door. The second I crossed the threshold, however, Anne's entryway made it extremely difficult for me not to feel thoroughly demoralized. The furniture and décor looked as if they had been purchased for a mid-priced hotel room. In Florida. Whitewashed wood and tropical pastels and paintings of flamingoes in all directions. "I have my appointments in my living room," Anne said, using the same arm-extended gesture she'd used initially.

"Please sit anywhere you like," she said while easing herself into a beautifully worn and comfortable-looking easy chair with two perfect throw pillows. I wanted *that* chair. *Her* chair. The only seat in the room that looked snug and welcoming and cozy and protective and like it was practically wagging its tail to greet you. I swear that had been my exact thought—that the chair was wagging its tail—when a dog, of sorts, poked its head around the corner. The dog appeared to be a canine version of his owner—tall and lanky to an extreme—and it proceeded to enter the room in extreme slow motion.

"Please do let me know if you mind Oscar joining us," Anne said. "No trouble at all to put him in the other room."

That seemed quite hard to believe, given the amount of time it had taken Oscar to negotiate the few steps that had brought him into the room. "No, no, by all means. I love dogs."

"He's very old. And deaf. He won't hear a word you're saying." Anne took a moment to chuckle at her own joke, during which time, Oscar toppled over sideways and thudded dramatically onto the floor. I gasped. "Oh no no, he's fine," Anne said. "Sorry that startled you. His joints are so stiff, that's just the way he lays down."

I had never been in any kind of therapy before and had only vague notions of how it was supposed to proceed based almost entirely on books and films, but this scene struck me as so spectacularly bizarre that I could not wait to put it in my next book.

Reassured by Anne and pleased with the notion that I had *already* acquired material for future writing, I glanced toward Oscar with an expression of warm affection. He was resting comfortably, as the saying goes. I felt my face fall, as the saying goes.

"Are you sure he's ok?" I asked. "Oscar, I mean?"

"I am *so* sorry he's such a distraction," Anne said as she leaned forward and looked at me with concentrated sincerity. "I *really* am. But if we could try to get started…let's talk about why you're here."

"Anne. I really don't think that Oscar is OK," I said.

Anne made a dismissive gesture with her hand. *"Of course, it's much easier to talk about the dog than the very difficult things in your own life—"*

"Anne. I'm pretty sure your dog is *dead.*"

Anne leaped up from her chair with impressive agility for an older woman and looked at Oscar, whose tongue could be seen poking out the side of his slightly-opened mouth. Anne started shrieking and wailing and moaning, let out one ear-splitting scream, and dissolved into hysterical sobs. I had no idea what I was supposed to do, so I sat in the chair for a while, a little sad that the scene had turned entirely too macabre for me to ever write about it.

I comforted her as best I could—fetched a box of tissues and made a couple of phone calls for her. I stayed until someone else arrived who could be with her and sort out the sad scene, and I took the whole occurrence as a sign. I never went back to therapy with Anne or with anyone else.

CHAPTER 5

IT WORKS DIFFERENTLY WITH OLD BODIES. ACHES AND PAINS and injuries of all varieties must be accommodated, those of the body and other kinds as well. Gino's body, my body—they are the cases that contain our history and allow us to tote it along from place to place.

Locations that once were lithe and yielding and moist have dried up like old bones in the desert. Locations that once were solid and sturdy and persuasive have grown loose and lazy, laying about as if they have earned a life of leisure. Favorite stances of bygone days have demanded to be put away in mothballs. Poses that brought great gasping breathless afternoons have been trotted out and tried, but have proven impossible with the accumulated array of surgery scars, adhesions, prosthetic joints.

Everything works differently with old bodies. The memories of the seamless lovemaking where Liam's and my bodies moved agilely and organically in the creation of call-and-response melting melding will remain in the treasure box of time. Now, there are fits and starts. Continual adjustments for a flair of pain here, an ache or cramp there. Things slide out that are meant to remain inside.

In other words, I can no longer avoid a loud, prolonged, symphonic fart from escaping at the moment that I begin to have a really good time. In other words, an orgasm. I suppose if I were a more dignified person, I would hold back and thus…hold back. Gino would be devastated, however, as he thinks my farts—at such a time—are purely marvelous. He considers this the most intimate thing any partner has ever shared with him. And, as this is a recent occurrence for me, it is a part of me that I have never shared with another before him.

On the rare occasions when the passage of voluminous gas does not accompany my orgasm, Gino is woefully disappointed. Discouraged and self-blaming. "Was it something I did?" Gino will ask. "Did you enjoy yourself?"

I think to myself: well, isn't this an extremely odd turn of events? Women have been reassuring men since the beginning of time that everything is all right even when they don't quite get to the finish line of orgasm. But, what about when they do get to the finish line, but don't put the final exclamation point on the fact with the fart accompaniment? I would think the cacophony of other noises that I make would be reassurance enough, but Gino is inconsolable without the final coup de grâce that in any other context would be utterly graceless.

And whereas all of this is, in fact, truth, it is also, of course, a metaphor.

Aches and pains and injuries and scars are everywhere, a long lifetime of them. A minefield everywhere you turn.

How is it that Gino can so blithely believe in the prospect of a good and solid future? From where does his faith come, that some hypothetical sum the two of us can build will be greater than the total of its—of our—broken parts?

CHAPTER 6

GINO WAS FOND OF SAYING THAT, BACK IN THE DAY, HE COULD navel-gaze with the best of them. He did his time in therapy, he said. No reason to go there again. Ancient history, he said. The first time he ever said this—the first time he told me the story of his childhood—was when I named him Gino.

It was just a few months after we had started dating, and we were sitting in the outdoor courtyard of a Mexican restaurant named Los Sombreros. The restaurant adopted a charmingly minimalist approach to its decorating—a plant here, a serape there. Los Sombreros let the delight of being enfolded in an entirely enclosed stone patio, seemingly a world apart from the surrounding inner city, stand as its own naked magic. Until that dinner I had called him J, which was short for Jacob, which wasn't his real name in the first place, as it turned out.

Yaakov, which *was* the original name of the person sipping his margarita in between enormous handfuls of freshly fried tortilla chips, had been born into a quiet, studious Jewish family. An only child, five-year-old Yaakov had been dropped off with the family across the street one afternoon so his mother could meet his father downtown and help him pick out a new winter coat. The beautiful camel coat still sat in its department store box—wrapped in tissue and tied with an ornate gold ribbon—when the bodies of his parents were pulled from the crumpled car.

As the daylight slipped away, police officers went door-to-door in Yaakov's neighborhood, searching for people who might know more about the tragic, deceased couple. His adopted Mama told him the story over and over—how Papa had taken one look at the officers' faces and ushered them into the kitchen to deliver whatever awful news they obviously had, how she had shrieked so loudly that all four daughters stopped in their tracks, how she fell to her knees and sobbed into her gingham apron, still holding the worn wooden spoon from the pasta sauce she had been stirring. But she did not sob for long. She stood up, placed the spoon carefully on the kitchen counter, tore off her apron, wiped her face and declared that the boy was now part of their family. "No different than if he came from my own womb like our girls," she said. She gave thanks to God, turned to her husband and said, "We have a son, Tony."

When Yaakov sat down to his first spaghetti dinner that night, his new Mama said, "I think maybe we call you Jacob now. I think you feel you fit in better with us, yes?"

In that single afternoon, Yaakov went from being Yaakov, the only child in a modest, restrained, little Jewish family, to being Jacob, the adopted child of the boisterous, argumentative, demonstrative Italian family across the street. Jacob looked around the table at his four sisters—Rosa, Gabriella and twins Anita and Angela—not exactly sure how much the new name would help him blend in. He was a fair-haired beanpole of a boy in a family of round, olive-skinned, dark brunettes. He told me he'd secretly wished they had given him an entirely new name—an Italian name—but he felt too guilty and disloyal to his birth parents to ever bring it up.

I have been continually both fascinated and humbled by real human beings. As a lifelong writer, it had become easy to get lost in my own head, in a world of created characters and the invented situations that revealed those characters' inner lives. And then, sitting across the table from me at Los Sombreros, I was confronted with a man whose history contained an unexpected twist that was both singular and poignant. His history was horrifying, and it was lovely. I realized I did not possess the imagination to have dreamed it up.

"Gino," I say to him. "From now on, I will call you Gino."

Even if I had not had my recent phone conversation with Pippa, I would not have had to dig very deeply to come up with that Italian name. It had been hovering around in my head for years, ever since Pippa kept me breathless with the details of her brief-but-rapturous tryst with Gino the Italian Sculptor.

I had probably been a widow for nearly a decade when Pippa's Gino encounter occurred. Pippa and I saw one another regularly, maintained a steady stream of contact, and kept close track of the myriad details of one another's lives. Pippa had gone to her usual Friday yoga—a candlelight class that often marked the highlight of her entire week. Pippa was hugely disappointed when her beloved instructor asked the group to welcome a guest instructor who had recently completed his training. She prepared herself to resent the interloper unequivocally, but she found herself craning her neck as the man wended his way to the front of the room and unrolled his mat. "Oh, my lord," Pippa thought, "It's David." Not as in David, a person that she had known previously. David, as in the statue "David." Michelangelo's "David."

When he introduced himself to the class as Gino, in a very slight accent, Pippa remained resolved to dislike him; but his Renaissance looks and bashful, self-effacing manner made it difficult. He had grace. He had lithe strength. He had a mop of curly hair and a shy smile. Pippa told me that she was panting when she asked Gino if he might like to go for coffee at the end of the class, and she flatly acknowledged that the panting was most definitely not from the exertion of the yoga moves. While waiting in line for their espressos, Pippa was nearly undone by the length and thickness of his eyelashes. Shortly after they had ensconced themselves at an out-of-the-way table, Gino was telling her that sculpture was his first love, his real love, and that each summer he travelled back to Carrera to painstakingly select individual pieces of marble that he would ship back to the United States to sculpt. He needed to examine the exact grain of the pieces. He needed to touch the marble with his two hands. He needed to feel the connection to his people while he felt the connection to their land, to the transformation of northern Tuscany that went back to the Early Jurassic period—190 million years ago—when large parts of the area were flooded, and lime sediment that had been deposited on the sea bottom first formed a carboniferous platform that ultimately became Carrera marble.

Pippa had been my best friend for a long time. When she told me this story, I challenged myself to figure out the exact moment in this encounter when Pippa began mentally ripping off Gino's clothes, and her own, unable to think of anything else but his marble-stroking body thrashing around with hers. I calculated that it was pretty much the moment he first mentioned going to Carrera to connect with his native marble. By caressing it between his two hands. I was wrong. She unabashedly confessed that it was essentially when he had unfurled his yoga mat at the beginning of the class, backlit by the candles in an amber aura.

The union of Pippa and Gino consisted of one long weekend. Pippa, blessedly, did not go into detail as she was sometimes wont to do. Dear Pippa. I think she actually believed she was being wholly subtle in her fervent and continued attempts to stir me into reopening whatever portal had enabled me to find Liam. No details were needed. The way she looked— for quite a time after that one weekend—spoke quite clearly. Her entire being was different. Her coloring remained ruddy. She seemed to fit more easily into both her own skin and the world at some deep-rooted level.

It made its impression on me—Pippa's story of Gino—and Pippa's own temporary transformation into a woman who had blossomed into a fuller self. I suppose you could say that my swiftness in christening Yaakov/Jacob/J with the new nickname was my own version of a prayer, my supplication to the universe for our own future, the newly-christened Gino's and mine.

Gino says that his childhood with his new family was spent largely in a state of extreme bewilderment. Years of it, he says. But then, he says that he would describe his first five years essentially the same way. When I've pressed him to tell me any memories of his first home and birth parents and early life, he maintains that all he can conjure up is a general impression of silence, a lot of bobbing up and down on the part of his father, and a great deal of time on his mother's part devoted to getting the yarmulke to remain in its proper place on his head. Otherwise, Gino says, it's a blur of black-and-white snapshots that float around in his brain. A checked shirt he wore. The slight furrow on his mother's brow as she stood over the stove and prepared their meals.

On occasion, and generally out of the blue, when Gino and I sat together reading, he would put down his newspaper and say something like, "You know, I'm pretty sure I was thinking of the shirt that Timmy was wearing when Lassie got trapped in the well." I, of course, stared at him blankly because there was absolutely no context for this comment whatsoever. He would then register surprise that I, apparently, had not clued into his train of thought—a train that he had picked up from a conversation that occurred days, or even weeks, ago. He would snap his paper and resume reading. "The point is," Gino would say, "I'm not certain if my memories are real at all, or if they're snippets of TV shows that I watched. Or photographs that I've seen. Possibly even photographs of someone else's family entirely!" As a writer whose work has been consumed with themes of loss and hope, this pained me deeply to hear. Gino had such little sense of his own life story—which was rife with loss and hope. It was as if every time he turned around to glimpse what lay behind him, the landscape he had traversed had already disappeared. Perhaps what pained me even more was Gino's attitude about that absence. It could not have mattered less to him. "The point is," he would say again, "why navel gaze about the past when you can't even be certain if anything that you quote remember unquote is quote real unquote."

Hence, Gino had repeatedly made it clear that there would be no "navel gazing," as he liked to put it. I supposed that could be fine by me. I supposed that I could try to make it fine. Certainly, it would be a world apart from what Pippa had described as Liam and me being "inside one another's bodies." At that point in my long life, I supposed that if I wanted to delve deeply into the feelings of another human being, I could invent a character and imbue him or her with all kinds of thorny personality traits, problematic family history, obscure motivations and thwarted ambitions. In the real world, I could sip margaritas, admire the plants and comment on the surprising lack of sombreros for a place named Los Sombreros.

Perhaps I could do this.

CHAPTER 7

BEFORE THERE WAS LANGUAGE, BEFORE THERE WAS WRITING, the earliest humans told stories.

More than fifteen thousand years ago, early people fashioned hollow tubes from wood, bone and plants. They pulverized rocks and seeds and berries to create pigments. Using the tubes they had made, they blew their pigments against vast cave walls that served as their canvasses. They dug and gouged at the walls to engrave them, to add to the story they wished to tell. One of these immense groupings of cave art came to be called Lascaux, the best known of more than three hundred fifty similar settings where stories were conveyed in pictures.

Before I could write, I told stories. I drew pictures with my box of crayons and made scribbles that I pretended were real words, and I read my little books to my mother.

For sixty-four years, stories swirled around within me. They were my constant companions. They circled in my head, and when they had taken enough shape inside of me, I wrote them down.

That reading I did—where my intentionally forgotten past and my ambivalently weighed future crossed paths in the forms of Tom Killarney and Gino Delvecchio—was the last event on that particular book tour. *Stony Ground,* my most recent novel, had been out in the world for nearly a year. I should have been well into writing a new book by then. I should have long ago stopped doing readings and events for *Stony Ground.* I should have halted my unseemly clinging and clawing for every last scrap of admiration and validation that affirmed what I had ceased to believe—that I was, in fact, a writer.

But I couldn't. I couldn't move on because the stories had stopped.

They had simply vanished.

I moved from room to room in my home. For days, for weeks, I did this. I sat in different chairs, at different desks and tables. I tried out both the east view and the west. Eventually, I ended up on the couch. I sat on that couch, and I resolved to not move until a story—a skeleton of a story, the outline of a character who may later tell a story, any kernel whatsoever—gathered itself from the gray nothingness and gave me the barest hint that something would take shape.

I had been a writer all my life. I could not understand what had happened.

I sat on the couch. I scratched at tiny particles of dried food on the upholstery. I switched from the velvet pillow to the chenille one, giving each one a number of sturdy punches to fluff the filling—also tremendously helpful in releasing all kinds of pent-up internal disturbances. Once, I sat for long enough that I wondered if I had actually become paralyzed, that I no longer had the ability to make any part of my body move. This began to seem possible to me. It seemed like an explanation: of course, I could not write. I could not write, because I could not move!

In other words, I had sunk into a state of extreme desperation. The essential core of how I understood who I was within the world had disappeared into a dense and ceaseless fog.

Tom Killarney.

Gino Delvecchio.

Perspective is everything. On a steep downward slope, you can feel as if you are flying. The world sails away as you rush through it. Going up that same slope, you see only the ground in front of your feet, ground that slips away into nothingness as you try to catch sight of the peak; but you cannot—not the barest glimpse of the top.

I had always thought of my first year of college as the worst year of my life. The year that I was robbed three times. The year that I had a stalker, before we had the word or the concept of such a thing. The year I flirted with the temptation of drowning my sorrows in alcohol as a possible future plan. The year I finally acknowledged that my father did not die when I was five years old, not in the way my mother had always said, anyway. The year I finally told my mother that I knew, that I had always known what really happened.

And then, so many years later, someone came to a book reading and told me that I changed the course of his life that year. That same year. That worst-year-of-my-life year.

It was neither failure nor lapse that I did not recognize Tommy Killarney. The man who came to my reading bore almost no similarity to the eighteen-year-old boy I had known. The lanky awkwardness, the exuberant puppy quality, even the prominent Adam's apple—gone. In their place was a solid, stocky body that had expanded in all directions, much the same as Dr. McClelland's nurse Ruth had done. Though I had never thought that Tommy talked particularly rapidly, the man who spoke to me at my reading had a cadence that was markedly slower, his pitch, a few gradations deeper. Most surprising of all, though, was that I could not see Tommy in the older Tom's smile.

Am I so changed as this?

"But who can remember pain, once it's over? All that remains of it is a shadow, not in the mind even, in the flesh. Pain marks you, but too deep to see. Out of sight, out of mind." Margaret Atwood wrote that.

Why journey into the faraway mists of so much time gone by? Memory is the very slipperiest of slippery slopes. A dark path. A bad road. A bold mess, is memory. A trickster shape-shifter seducer that swindles us into believing that we know our own past, that we possess the things that have happened to us in a storehouse of trustworthy information.

Who can remember pain, once it's over?

The events, whatever they may have been, have gotten whittled and magnified and repackaged and woven into an ongoing narrative, the story I hold of my own life. Each time a memory has traversed the synaptic space from my deepest wells back into my everyday thoughts, the tale has amended anew. Adjusted, altered, eroded, embellished.

I cannot remember that year. Robbery. Stalker. Drinking. Even the truth about my father. Those are items on a list; memories don't accompany them. I worked to forget, jettisoned large chunks of that year, like the icebergs of vomit breaking from my wall and crashing to the ground. Nothing remains but a torn snapshot here, a few seconds of grainy film that gets stuck in the projector there.

I cannot remember that person. The eighteen-year-old version of me. I have lost whatever bridges there have been in the forty-six years that spanned the expanse between Esmé then and me now.

I have lost myself.

Who can remember pain, once it's over?

I cannot remember her, but perhaps I can get inside of her, *inhabit* her, *be* her for that one year of my life—in much the same way Pippa imagined that I inhabited Liam.

Perspective is everything.

Perhaps it's worth going back there, revisit that time. Perhaps going back is the best way forward, the path to unblocking the things that have been frozen—the words, the stories.

You're thinking: but wait, you've already given it away. You've told us everything that happened that year. Ah, but stories are never about the *events*. Never.

FALL 1972
TO
FALL 1973

"'Are you at all acquainted with squalor?'"

—J.D. Salinger
"For Esmé—with Love and Squalor"

CHAPTER 8

THERE WAS A CERTAIN PLACE I SAT IN MY BEDROOM WHEN I pored over the catalogs and brochures that different colleges sent me. It was the only time that I ever sat there, on the floor, huddled in the little corner between the bed and the desk and the door to my closet, almost as if I were hiding.

From the middle of my junior year on, it felt like I was receiving invitations into a strange and mysterious world that I knew nothing about. I ran my fingers across the textured paper of the catalog covers, examined the typefaces they had chosen to represent their schools, scanned the pictures of students who looked like they were simultaneously intently serious and having a wonderful time. I had no idea how colleges had gotten my name and my home address, which added to the mystique. Not long before the college barrage began, I also started receiving tons of material from the John Birch Society, a radical right group who was somehow convinced that I would make an excellent candidate to join their ranks. It was so utterly off the mark that it rattled me. I actually wondered if they had some secret knowledge of my deep inner workings that I didn't possess myself. The whole thing was bewildering, especially when they sent me their full, published manifesto—

imprinted in gold with my name. The John Birchers had my name and address; and they had singled me out, which had engendered a suspicion of *anyone* who sent me something in the mail that invited me to learn the secret handshake and be ushered into their unique brand of sorcery.

As was my habit, I thought about the Kimball family. They were my lodestone, my North Star. The oldest Kimball boy was smart; he'd been an exceptional student and had an all-around great high school record. When it was time for him to go to college, he didn't look past our home state of Pennsylvania. No one did where I came from. There were a million colleges to choose from as well as the big state university, and desiring to reach further than the many options at hand seemed ungrateful somehow, a muddle of priorities. I pondered and weighed the magnitude of options about my future in secret, in the corner of my room.

Mom was pretty stealth-like when she made her way down the carpeted hallway to my bedroom, but I always knew when she was on her way. I had plenty of time to gather all the college brochures and pack them away in the bottom of my lowest dresser drawer. When Mom swung my door open after a quick, perfunctory knock, I'd be lounging casually on my bed leafing through a magazine or—more likely—gazing intently at the latest paperback novel I was reading.

I put my index finger into the book to hold my place, and said something like, "I gave up on *Atlas Shrugged*. Couldn't care less about John Galt. I'm never reading anything by that crazy lunatic Ayn Rand again." Mom and I never said regular stuff like, "Hi, what are you up to?" or things of that sort. We started right in. I always had a snippet of conversation prepared. I wasn't especially good at improvising, and I needed a ready-made opening line.

Mom sat on the corner of my bed whenever she came in. She crossed her ankles. Always. Very proper-like. My girlfriends' moms got right up on the bed with them, just like they were teenagers themselves. Sometimes the other mom would plop right down with their head on a pillow—even when I was there—the three of us crowded together and lined up in a row, staring at the ceiling and gabbing. It felt strange and awkward, kind of like I was doing something forbidden because it felt so *casual*. I'd go through a list in my head of all the things that were wonderful and special about Mom and me until I could feel myself Scrooge up inside and get critical about my friends' mothers. I admit it. I was jealous. But it had been just Mom and me since the night my dad died when I was five years old, and she had to figure everything out.

Let's see. Minimum of two times a week, every week, since my dad met his demise, that I had heard my mom say it: that a woman had to work twice as hard, be twice as good. That it was a man's world, through and through. That to even get noticed, a woman had to be extraordinary, unfailingly so, whereas a man could be completely average (sub-par was my mother's phrase) and still grab the world by the tail. That made 1,352 times that I'd had that idea repeated to me. It had been twelve years since the unexceptional mid-March day when my father left for work and never returned.

"I thought you really loved *The Fountainhead!*" she said.

"I did. But I'm seriously considering changing my mind and denying that I ever said that. Rand seems like such a runaway, capitalist *bitch*. She and the other very special, brilliant, talented people whom she believes get to do pretty much whatever they want in order to achieve their full, dazzling potential. *Bitch!*" I said again, for emphasis.

Mom re-crossed her ankles. "Seriously, Esmé, are you going to swear this much at college?"

That one stopped me in my tracks. Mom and I had been doing the dance for months, honoring a mutual agreement that had never been discussed. The one where we both went about our lives same as ever and more or less pretended that—even though I was a senior in high school—nothing was about to change.

That was why I read the college material all huddled over and cramped into a corner of my room. Like I was hiding. I *was* hiding.

I was also torn.

I kept reading catalogs.

I got caught up in the picture.

I had always wanted to be a writer; that's the reason I got interested in That School. A school that everyone knew the name of, which was more of a negative thing to me than a positive. I had always thought of the school as a bastion of the Establishment—weren't the power of wealth and privilege and the whole Establishment that they had constructed exactly what we'd all been protesting and organizing and struggling to dismantle? But the college had a special program for people who knew, right from the beginning, that they wanted to major in English literature. That was the closest you could come to studying writing in those days—you could become an English major and take as many creative writing courses as you could cram in along the way. No more than ten people were accepted into this English program each year. Those ten embarked on a double credit, year-long journey with a single professor for their entire freshman year.

Like I said, I got caught up in the picture.

I imagined myself hunched over a worn, time-darkened wood desk that generations of eager students had used before me. I would be accompanied by the gentle hum of my Sears portable electric typewriter, bolstered and enthused by continuous cups of rich, black coffee. I would dream up characters as iconic as Chief Broom and Nurse Ratchett in *One Flew Over the Cuckoo's Nest.* I would send the characters on journeys as epic as those of Jean Valjean in *Les Misérables.* I would devise endings as satisfying as those of Charles Dickens, but with structure and prose as thrillingly *avant garde* as Virginia Woolf.

I would find my voice. I would ferret it out from the bricks and the stone and the ivy. I would find my voice, and I would let it sing.

"We considered it a wasted year if we didn't get at least one marriage proposal," my mother said. Out of nowhere. "Which we rejected, of course. It didn't count if it was a proposal that you actually considered."

Even though it was one of the rare times that my mother and I talked about college *at all,* I can't say that this particularly matched my own idea of "talking about college." I'm sure I looked at her as if she had sprouted a second head.

"You know, we Tri-Delts, I meant," as if that cleared up everything. It was an amazing fact that my mother invariably seemed to be leafing through a magazine when she said miscellaneous things like this—a magazine she had brought home from Dr. McClelland's office, usually accompanied by a retelling of the story of my name. Again.

"You're seriously saying that it was a *goal* to have a man propose to you? Every year?"

"At least one. Yes," she said and batted her eyes at me playfully.

"That's exceptionally weird. And sad," I said.

"You're being so serious. Times were different."

"Different in that people didn't get their hearts broken by being completely spurned in love, or different in that people proposed marriage without any love in the first place?" I asked.

I predicted the great heaving sigh well before it came. She said, "You live in such a serious world, Esmé. I was just talking about college. The fun. The lightness of those friendships with my sorority sisters."

"I'm pretty sure it's my seriousness that got their attention," I said. "You know, the poem about death and all."

Show me nothing of death
Let no track cross my path

Not one shadow of
the baby bird as it
Falls from its nest
Never to know to feel to
Fly

Not one outline of
the worm who
Curled and dried on the sidewalk
Unable to reclaim
Earth

Not one wave-tossed shell
on an unspoiled beach
The disconnected shield
A creature of the
Sea

Not a chair
Especially not a chair
The hollow of your body
The fabric stain from your arms
Empty

Show me nothing of death
Let no track cross my path

I wrote that poem in creative writing class sometime in
the middle of junior year. My teacher Mrs. Baumann asked
my permission to "drop it in the bucket"—her expression for
adding it to her file of students' works that she submitted to
various publications and contests. She asked everybody that

all the time, with the same sheepish and proud smile on her face every time. Mrs. Baumann had a mop of curly, bright red hair, gigantic eyeglasses, and awkward orthopedic shoes. She looked as if she ought to be a beloved character in a classic children's book, and I loved her for her unwavering enthusiasm toward our writing efforts. I loved her in general. I said sure, she could "drop it in the bucket," and I never really thought about it again. A few months later she told me that the poem had been chosen for publication in a new high school English textbook, in the section on free verse poetry. I was proud, I suppose, but already had my sights set on getting out of high school and moving into the greater world beyond Clarion, Pennsylvania. I couldn't muster a whole lot of enthusiasm for it. I was stunned when colleges started sending me letters congratulating me on the poem and its publication and inviting me to apply. It briefly sent me back to my earlier quasi-paranoia about the John Birch Society having a cache of secret information about me. But Mrs. Baumann explained that she'd had to submit a lot of information about me along with the submission, including which colleges I might be interested in applying to. There's just always a lot going on behind the curtain; I certainly knew that already.

"Mom. How come you never dated anyone? After Daddy died, I mean."

My mother often did this thing, a gesture that was completely her own, where she tilted her chin very slightly. It meant that whatever question had been posed, or direction the conversation had veered into, she preferred not to respond. Strongly preferred. But she felt that she had to, for the sake of decorum and not appearing rude, which trumped all else.

She continued to leaf through the pages of her magazine, and she did not look up at me.

"Well, I suppose it never really occurred to me. I had you to raise," she said.

"I remember the way Daddy looked at you. I remember it. He loved you so much. He *saw* you," I said. "Didn't you want to have that again?"

Whereas it was rare for my mother to talk about college, I had ventured into even more perilous waters. It was unheard of for her to talk about that other subject—my father's death. She did not tilt her chin, nor did she respond.

It was not so long after that conversation that I awakened to a thin dusting of snow one early April morning. The spring flowers that had already made their appearance looked as if they were bowing their heads, just a nod. They looked as if they were sad, desolated by this uninvited return of winter. But the sun had already broken through before I had finished getting ready for school—the lush, bright sun that trumpets the arrival of warmer, sunnier, better days ahead.

No evidence of winter's fickle ending remained when I got home from school that afternoon and opened our mailbox to its familiar, rusty creak. I withdrew the envelope, and I saw the name of the school. The thin, letter-sized envelope. Translucently thin and bright white, with embossed lettering in a typeface that suggested solidity, sobriety and importance.

I tapped the letter against the side of the mailbox a couple of times, sort of like shaking a present to guess what might be inside. I held it up to the April sun. One thin sheet of paper inside, folded into thirds, with two or three paragraphs of text. I went inside the house, sat down at the dining room table, and put the letter squarely in front of me while I imagined what it would say. "Dear Fill-in-the-Blank Name, We regret to inform you…" Or maybe, "We had a record number of exceptionally well-qualified applicants this year…"

Everyone knew what the arrival of a thin envelope meant. The fat envelope was the one you wanted, the one that signaled you had been accepted. The thin one meant rejection.

I sat at the table staring at that envelope for a long time. I forced myself to picture the beautiful, enormous campus of the state university that Mom and I had visited, and I tried to envision myself there, walking under the canopy of towering maple trees. I thought about The Engineers whom I'd spent the evening with, and I smiled. When I had filled myself up with enough good memories from my visit and recalled stories I'd heard from older kids I'd known who had gone there, I felt ready to open the envelope and see exactly what gently rueful words the *other* college—the college I would *not* be attending—had used to announce the dashing of my future dreams.

I supposed I was angry, seeing as how I ripped the envelope into a wrinkled mess when I tore into it. The letter took a pretty good hit, too. The letter that announced I was one of the ten people who had been accepted into the special program in English Literature. I needed to read the letter a second time, and then a third.

My high school made a big deal of me being the first student ever to be accepted to this college. I'm pretty sure that I may have been the first person who had ever applied. In many ways, I embraced—and even idealized—the life of small pleasures and measured dreams. It was a big stretch for me to think about applying to this college in the first place. I couldn't even begin to picture what it might really be like to be so far away, in so many different ways, from anything I had experienced.

I suppose there was no way I could have imagined any of that in advance, nor any of the accumulation of catastrophes that one year brought, even if I had read the fine print. Besides, whatever foreknowledge I might have been able to glean would likely not have dissuaded me from my secret hope: that with all of those smart kids, those Big Brains, perhaps there would be one who could truly see me. See *me*. Just one.

CHAPTER 9

MOM SURPRISED ME THE MORNING OF OUR TRIP TO COLLEGE with a brand-new towel set (a hideous pop art mess of two-tone pink flowers, but the towels did kind of match the crazy and now ancient bathrobe she had made me), a toaster, and two packages of Pop Tarts in my favorite flavors (blueberry and brown sugar cinnamon). She had not said a word; the new gifts were simply sitting at the foot of my bed when I woke up. Santa Claus, tiptoeing in the night.

Clarion, Pennsylvania had a population of about six thousand people. The eighty miles between us and the city of Pittsburgh may as well have been a thousand. Mom and I had gone to the Big City a handful of times, and most of those visits were when I was a very small child. My few memories were dim and fuzzy: A horrifically stinky zoo with animals pacing back and forth in tiny cages. A paper placemat in the shape of a cow that lay underneath my first chocolate milk shake. I held the freezing concoction that was not quite liquid and not quite solid in my mouth while I swung around on the bright red stool. *The Sound of Music* on a screen so immense that I felt pressed back in my seat by a barrage of pictures and sounds—I had nightmares about the Baroness' nostrils and the way the peals of thunder rattled inside of my chest. Mostly, I remember walking down the sidewalks of the city streets, my mother gripping my hand so tightly that it hurt a little. Pittsburgh seemed both too crowded and too empty. So much rushing, so little life.

Mom and I had made one trip to Washington, D.C., but I was really young for that trip as well. We stayed with a friend of Mom's named Heidi. My mom and Heidi had known each other since they were best friends at Clarion High. All I could really remember of Washington was another foul-smelling zoo and the inside of the friend's apartment. Heidi bought me a balloon at the zoo, bright white with pink silhouettes of animals marching in a circle all around the center. The balloon floated in the air all by itself. Heidi wrapped the long string around and around my wrist and tied it in a knot. While she and my mother talked and talked, I marveled at my floating balloon and said the names of the animals over and over again to myself: rhi-noc-er-os, el-e-phant, gi-raffe, go-ril-la, fla-min-go.

I remembered the exact hue of the pale grey-blue carpeting in Heidi's apartment, the wrought-iron railing along the two stairs that linked the living room and the dining room, the gleaming black of her baby grand piano. The city itself left no lasting impression.

I did not have a whole lot of urban experience, in other words; but the city where my new college resided had a population of fewer than 150,000 people. I didn't think of it as any kind of big deal, not something that would be utterly unknown to me.

My mom had gotten a gigantic road map to plan for our trip. Even though the majority of the seven-hour drive was a straight shot across Interstate 80 followed by one other major interstate, we marked the entire route with a thick red magic marker line across our map before we set out that morning. I also had some official literature from the college that included a detailed map of the route from the interstate exit to the campus itself. It looked like the route went straight through the downtown area and that the campus lay pretty much in the exact center of the city. I wrote out the specific directions to my freshman dorm on a sheet of paper, including the closest place to park for unloading and moving in.

The drive was weirdly reminiscent of the trip Mom and I had taken to the state university for my one college visit. Searching around for radio stations with the least static. Mom turning the car air conditioning higher when she got too hot, me turning it down when I got too cold. I'm dying. I'm freezing. I need to pee. I need something cold to drink. This is literally the worst cup of coffee I've had in my entire life. That was about the extent of the conversation. It seemed like no time at all passed. It seemed like ages passed.

"Here's our exit," Mom said. "Ready or not, college, we're a-comin' for ya."

Game was the word that came to mind. Mom was being game. Pretending that nothing especially special was happening and keeping such an entirely light tone that I swear I could feel my heart shift a little in my chest, trying to find a safe place so it wouldn't just squeeze up and break.

We left the high-speed languor of the interstate to find our-selves in the outskirts of a town where the tidy little houses and manicured lawns could have been anywhere at all. A comforting, but creepy, anonymity.

We passed through an area of vast concrete nothingness, abandoned warehouses surrounded by enormous parking lots, the cracks in the pavement so longstanding that weeds as tall as sunflowers had claimed their patches of earth. We passed the corner of one such parking lot, and BAM, it was as if we had been dropped into the center of city. A kind of city. A movie set version of a city. A beautiful old brick building that had been carefully and tastefully renovated right next door to an urban wreck of a shop with bars and grates and pad-locks and chains running every which way, right next door to some business that had been abandoned and was now home to graffiti, posters, sale notices and missing-dog flyers glued one on top of the other, the whole accumulation dissolving into a pentimento. A corner park with lush green grass and dazzling flower beds. At the next corner, a park strewn with trash and broken bottles, the neglected benches bleached to the same gray as the concrete, all of them missing planks from their seats. The late August sun dancing off the shards of bro-ken glass and setting them on flashes of fire.

We passed a well-dressed middle-aged woman holding the leash of her cute little dog in one hand; in the other hand, she clenched a baseball bat.

Mom and I looked at one another. Without a word, she pulled the car over to the curb and reached her hand out toward me. The map. She wanted to check the map again. She studied it, looked through the dashboard to the street signs at the intersection, and touched her index finger to our exact location. She set the map down and began driving again.

I finally broke the silence. "Squalor," I said.

"For Esmé—with Love and," Mom said.

"I think this is a different kind."

"A kind with beautiful old elm trees framing it," she said.

"Mom. Seriously," I said. "The woman with the baseball bat. Do you think it's safe here?"

Her smile was weak. "About as safe as anywhere, I suppose," she said. "It's a pretty fancy school, after all. Right?"

It sure did not seem like we could possibly be close to a university, let alone on the edge of the campus itself, as the map indicated we were.

CHAPTER 10

It hadn't registered with me that the entire freshmen class was housed on a campus that stood separate from the rest of everything. Meaning, along the edges of a monstrous quadrangle, a vast sea of grass that was crisscrossed by a network of pathways. Meaning, a killingly long distance from the closest place that we could park. My mom pulled up to the curb at the end of a long line of cars lit up with emergency flashers blinking in a dazzling display of oranges and reds. She gave me another weak-but-brave-smile, and we opened the doors of her little red station wagon to a day that would go on record as one of the most wretchedly hot days I ever experienced. Meltingly, inexcusably hot. Like opening the car door and being under water. When that stifling wall of air hit me, I had the thought for the first time: This school was trying to crush me. Right from that moment of my very first day, I began to fear that school itself was chasing my soul.

I had that thought even before I learned that my dorm room —Wren Hall Room 545—was on the fourth floor, the fourth floor of a building that had no elevator. And there was a flight of stairs up to the "first" floor. I was not even slightly charmed by the European sensibility of this, though I was awestruck by the staircase that rose in front of me. The stairs appeared to be genuine white marble, and the once-sharp corners of the steps, still visible at each stair's edge, had worn and rounded into smooth curves at the middle. The footfalls of generations who had come before me. I stood in humbled awe.

Still, I was crestfallen that such a thing as a fourth-floor walk-up (that was actually a fifth-floor walk-up) was to be part of my new life, the path that would lay between me and the world outside. It was a dispiriting thought, and—not being an especially athletic person—I got the notion that I might be destined to spend a year planning my days around *not* returning to my dorm room more than I absolutely needed to. I feared that my avoidance of the climb may well imprison me, becoming an excuse to remain in my tower, to isolate myself even more than my usual.

In the meantime, my mom and I had to get the sundry possessions that filled the back of the station wagon up all of those stairs.

Thank heavens I was more or less of a minimalist. I hadn't brought all that much stuff.

Meaning, thanks heavens I was poor.

I had two large suitcases filled with clothes, my towels and linens, and a few boxes of miscellaneous…stuff. Two rolled up posters to decorate. And a brand-new toaster.

I said Hi! Hi! Hi! to all of my fellow freshmen and their family members as they lugged endless numbers of suitcases. I scanned the faces of my classmates for any hints to who they might be. I noted the high-end stereo equipment and the boxes with the names of stores I had only read about in novels or seen in ads within mom's cache of magazines. The families seemed impermeable to the heat. I surreptitiously checked their brows for beads of sweat. I inhaled as they passed, trying to catch a whiff of rank, locker-room-worthy sweat. My mother and I were dripping puddles well before we reached the top floor for the first time.

The stereo equipment, the store names, the careful way that the parents carried various lamps and desk accessories—it all seemed to paint a consistent picture. But nothing so much as their shoes. I looked at the shoes of my classmates' parents as they made their ways up and down the marble staircases with the lacquered ebony wood trim, and I felt pretty certain that I might very well be the only person in this group who was at this school on scholarship. A feeling of fierce pride and a wave of desolate loneliness welled up within me, side by side.

Shoes.

Shoes always made me think of Shirley.

Dear, dear Shirley. Shirley with her crazy Harpo Marx hair, coke-bottle-bottom-thick eyeglasses, and large spaces between each of her teeth. Shirley who never stopped smiling and laughing. Shirley who came to our house every week to help pay off her debt to Dr. McClelland. It was a set-up, and I knew it, and Mom knew it, too. Shirley couldn't pay her family's medical bills to Dr. McClelland, so he had suggested an arrangement where her family could get all of their medical care if Shirley did some cleaning and odd chores at both his house and my mother's. Dr. McClelland's family didn't really need the help—they had a cleaning person already, a woman who had been with his wife Sandy's family since Sandy was a little girl herself. But Dr. McClelland understood that Shirley needed the dignity of working for her medical care and that my mother could use an extra pair of hands since she worked full-time for him.

Mom would still be at work the days that I got home from school and Shirley was there at our house. She saved the tasks that allowed her to stay in one place—like ironing or folding the laundry—for the hour or so that we were together. Shirley's gap-toothed smile lit the room when I came in. Nobody else ever gave me that feeling—like I was so special and loved and fun that they were just bursting to see me. Nobody after my father died, anyway.

"Hey, Esmé, you're really not going to believe the deal that I got this time. Look at these shoes! Aren't they the cutest things ever? So comfortable, too. You're not going to believe it. Two pairs for $3.95. I'm pretty sure the sale is still going on. K-Mart. If you and your mom rush right over there, you can snag yourselves some. Don't forget: K-Mart. I know, I know. I'm usually pretty loyal to Zayre's, but K-Mart has some really great stuff, too.".

So often it was about shoes. The magnitude of her delight and pride about the treasure she had found. The joy in being able to spread the news to me. I oohed and ahhhed and hoped it never came to light that my mom refused to set foot in a K-Mart. She thought the store was "sub par." Mom scrimped and saved and pinched pennies six ways to Sunday, but she had her standards and drew her lines as well.

I stood on the landing of those hallowed, worn stairs and watched people's feet and looked at their fancy shoes, and I thought of the footfalls of generations past, and I thought of Shirley, and big, gloppy tears flooded my eyes. The staircase suddenly seemed a metaphor. I was moving in, and I was moving up. It was an entirely foreign world, and I wished more than anything that I had bought a pair of shoes for myself at Zayre's. I wanted to never forget who I was.

By about the fifth trip to the car and back—watching the swirl of humanity around me—I realized that I was going to be meeting a whole lot of people in a very short time. I decided that first impressions and snap judgements, which were a bad habit of mine in the first place, were going to be an absolute must. First one that came to mind: rich people do not seem to sweat.

At some point two young women came out of their first-floor room and introduced themselves as my resident advisors—Julia and Emily. One was quite tall and willowy and the other was quite tall and...not-so-willowy. I wondered if perhaps one of them had purposely gained weight so people may be able to tell them apart. They both had long, very blonde hair, oversized blue eyes, enormous toothy smiles, and eyebrows that were slightly raised in a perpetually expectant expression. I disliked them immediately, for no reason other than they seemed too similar to one another and too preternaturally

Scandinavian. I decided I wasn't going to even bother to remember which one was which.

When my mom and I got to the fourth/fifth floor landing the first time, I pulled the key from my pocket that I'd been given by the smiling Norse twins. The old brass key was engraved with the numbers "545," which I thought was a very handy system until I realized that anyone who may find my key, should I happen to lose it, could let themselves right in. I inserted my key into the beautifully worn lock of room 545. A little thrill ran through me, and a little panic as well, as I turned the key and pushed open the door to my new home— only the second home I was to have since my birth.

My mother and I walked slowly, almost as if we were hesitant to enter a stranger's house, a house that was not really ours, and we found ourselves in what I naturally assumed was my dorm room. The white-painted room had glorious dark wainscoting and crown molding and hardwood floors that matched the entry doors. There was a *fireplace* with a *mantle*. A *fireplace?* The fact that it was ornamental did not make the shock of finding this in *my dorm room* any less. Strangely, the room was virtually empty—one desk on the long wall opposite the mantle and a built-in window seat that ran the length of the leaded-glass windows. This space bore no resemblance to the featureless, institutional dorm rooms I had seen at Penn State.

The room was, in many ways, more grand than the home my mother and I had lived in my whole life.

Then, it struck me. Where were our beds? I was thoroughly confused.

A young woman popped out of a side door on the far side of the mantle. I had gotten a postcard from the school with the names of my two roommates, so I knew she was either Susan McDermott or Carrie Fishman. She introduced herself as Carrie Fishman and asked me if Julia and Emily had told me that Susan McDermott had decided at the very last minute to defer her admission.

"What?" I wasn't exactly sure what that meant, but I thought the bottom line was that Carrie would be my only roommate.

"Yeah," Carrie said. "So, that means we each have our own bedroom. Pretty cool, huh? I chose this one." Carrie pointed over her shoulder toward the side door she had emerged from.

"Our own *bedrooms?*" I blurted.

I looked over at Mom, who raised her eyebrows quite high but didn't say a word. In unison, Mom and I gazed toward the other side door, which I had originally thought must be a closet but now understood was to be my own private bedroom. We made our way toward the door in the same tentative manner that strongly suggested a mutual feeling of guilt and paused at the threshold to behold my tiny, but *private,* bedroom.

When Mom took a potty break, I popped into Carrie's bedroom to have a peek. Of course, she had arrived before I did. But from the look of it, Carrie seemed to have arrived weeks before, as her tiny bedroom already bore the appearance of having been lived in for a while. She had covered her walls with posters of two things: big cats, as in lions and jaguars and cougars, and huge tomb rubbings of medieval knights.

The rest of the room was decorated in a mishmash of floral prints not unlike my new towels—lampshades, throw pillows, sheets and blankets, all of which had different sizes and colors of flowers.

Carrie herself wore her clearly ornery hair parted with razor-like severity straight down the middle and braided in two tight braids. She had an overbite and kind of bad acne and looked both bewildered and ironic at once—an adorable combination of geeky and arch. She wore a plaid cotton shirt, and a quick peek into her closet revealed a seemingly un-limited supply of plaid cotton shirts. I liked her immediately.

When the last trip from the car to my new home had been made, my mother and I stood in the middle of my tiny room looking at one another. She reached out her arm and cupped my cheek with her hand. "I'm spent," she said. "OK if I go check in to my hotel and shower and cool off? Maybe even put my feet up for a while?"

"Sure," I said. "Of course."

"Or…do you want to come with me? Cool off yourself?" she asked.

Neither one of us knew what to do. It had always been the two of us. Just the two of us. We would be making it all up from here on. "No, might as well start to get unpacked. You know. Act like I'm going to be living here."

"All right," she said. "If you're sure." She turned to go, then turned back. "Oh, I was wondering if you wanted me to come back and take you out to dinner somewhere. But maybe you want to eat in the…what do they call the place where the students eat?"

"The dining hall. In keeping with the school's general refusal to call anything here by the usual name, like 'cafeteria,'" I said. "I read that in the orientation brochure they sent." My first day there, and the school was already making me feel weary.

"Dining hall. At any rate, we didn't talk about it—about what you might want to do."

I knew she was exhausted. I knew that the only hotel she could afford was pretty far out of town. "Guess I have to get used to the dining hall sooner or later. Guess I'll give it a try," I said.

CHAPTER 11

I WASN'T GOING ANYWHERE AT ALL. I WAS WALKING FROM ONE far corner of the quadrangle to the other, the longest distance between two arbitrary points, trying to locate some sense of anchoredness that had been sorely lacking. It was my third day at college. I had managed to wait that long to call Mom. Some crazy snafu meant that our dorm room telephones weren't working when we arrived, and they still weren't working three days later. I had gathered a boatload of change and waited in a sweltering line of wilted freshman to take my turn at the one and only remaining pay phone for a thousand brand-new students.

It was a painfully short call, during which both Mom and I mostly tried not to cry. I tried to be newsy. I tried to make her laugh. She let out a real belly laugh when I told her about the girl who had worn the same nightgown, combat boots and huge old army jacket every day so far, despite the record-breaking temperatures. I'd gotten the resounding Mom laugh I'd been most hoping for. I decided I'd better let the next person in line have their turn. Rip my own band-aid off and get back to the business of wandering and wondering what this entirely new world would bring.

My third day had passed exactly like the first two. Nonstop meetings, panels, discussions, information sessions (I mean, how much information is there?), etc., that the college had assembled for our orientation week. Perhaps they thought everyone would be consumed with homesickness as well as fear of the academic brutalities that lay ahead, but they kept us very *busy.* I felt like I was at some sort of summer camp where none of the activities made any sense. All of us freshman marched around to the places that our individualized schedules indicated, on time, with our notebooks open and our sharpened pencils in our hands. When the time for that particular activity was up, we gazed down at a solidly white page and were perplexed that there had been nothing whatsoever to record. Unless we doodled; then we had something to show for our time, at least.

I'd never known heat like that back home. Summers were humid where I came from, but not like this. I kept having the thought that if I stood still and held my arms out straight, the water would suck right out of the air and coat my arms and I would rain. My arms would rain.

It seemed as if the entire freshman class must be sprawled out on the vast lawn that evening, nearing the breaking point after the endless stream of unbearably hot evenings that festered throughout our entire first week. The ache to escape choking, airless dorm rooms that clutched the day's heat and refused to let it go gave real urgency to the need to flee, to lay our bodies down in the cool grass.

Piercing through my overheated daze, a voice rang out

from a fair distance: "Esmé! Hey, Esmé from…somewhere in Pennsylvania!"

I scanned the general direction that the shout seemed to have come from and saw a guy shoot up from the grass and proceed to wave two very long, very pale arms in the air as if he'd just had a horrible accident and was flagging down rescue. I hesitated, paralyzed with ambivalence about whether or not I had it in me to generate small talk with yet more unknown peers. He started up with the arm waving again, so— my ambivalence still intact—I navigated through the bodies of my fellow freshman and made my way toward him. There were a number of folks sprawled around him in a haphazard circle, each of whom had a red plastic cup filled with varying amounts of beer. Within a few short days, the college had sponsored an astonishing number of official receptions, and all of them offered unlimited, icy-cold kegs of beer. It appeared as if this school was as interested in teaching us to drink as it was in teaching us anything else.

"Oh, my God," I said. "Are you sitting there with the freshman directory seeing if you can recognize people from their tiny little pictures? And yelling out to them?"

He laughed. His Adam's apple bounced up and down on his long neck as he did, which I found completely disarmingly charming. "Well, yeah," he said. "I guess that's pretty much exactly what I'm doing. I'm Tom."

I took a quick glance at the motley group that surrounded him and said, "Did you start out by yourself tonight and gather this whole group of people already? That's pretty impressive!"

"Yeah, that's exactly right," Tom said. "Actually, not really. I've met most of them over the past few days. Dorm. Orientation stuff. Dining hall. Hey, Esmé, you're the first person I've ever known with that name. Not even sure I'm saying it right."

"You are," I said. "It's from a Salinger short story my mom was totally obsessed with. Not many people our age know it—the story, I mean—so no one's heard of the name."

"Read it." I swung my head toward the sound, which had come from the ground below Tom and me and sounded for all the world like a bullfrog croaking. I parsed together what the message had been.

"That's Tom," Tom said. "Hey, I should introduce you to everyone."

"His name is Tom, too?" I said to Tom #1, then swung my head around again and said, "You've read it? I grew up thinking that everyone in the world must know that story, but not one kid in my high school class had read it before I talked about it," to Tom #2. Another swing of the head and I said to Tom 1, "If all the rest of these folks are named Tom, that would be awesome. Easy to remember."

The other Tom stood up, with some effort, put his cigarette in his mouth, rubbed his hands together to shake loose the grass and dirt, and held his hand out for me to shake. "No, just me." He shook my hand, put the cigarette back in his hand after taking a very big drag, and plopped back down on the lawn.

"A handshake," I said. "Wow." I smiled at him and waited for him to talk, but he didn't say anything. I continued, "Anyway, I said a while back, 'You've read it?'"

" 'For Esmé—with Love and Squalor,' " Tom 2 said. "Yeah."

I waited for more, but there was nothing after that. Tom 2 took another deep drag from his cigarette. Tom 1 put his hands on his hips and looked up toward the heavens. Tom 2 gestured toward him with his cigarette and said, "He hates me. Well, to be fair, we probably hate each other. Equally."

"Wow," I said again. "That's quick work. How long have we all been here—is it three days now?"

"We went to the same high school," Tom 1 said. "We weren't really friends, but I don't think anyone actually hates anyone else."

"Ok…well…glad to hear that," I said. I felt as if I'd wandered in during the last act of a play and was laboring to piece together a story from the endgame. I also felt exceptionally awkward, and I wondered—if I had gone to dinner just a little earlier or been at a slightly different place in line for the payphone—might I have avoided this whole scene.

"Different crowds. Different friend groups. We didn't really know each other very well," Tom 1 said. "By the way, people pretty much call me Tommy. That might avoid confusion."

"Thank God," I laughed. "I was getting worried about telling you guys apart. Nightmares of the twins Lynn and Linda in my class back home. I knew them from kindergarten; end of high school, I still couldn't tell them apart. Not for the life of me. Really pissed them off."

"Different crowds. Right. Then we drove here together." It was Tom 2 who said that, and with his words, he shot a highly withering look at Tom 1. "Longest eight hours of my entire fucking life."

Tom 1 laughed heartily, as if this was genuinely funny and we were all enjoying mirthful, lighthearted banter. Tom 2 again sprang up with the same startling suddenness, jabbed a finger in my direction, and said, "Want a beer? I'm going to get more."

It was that exact time of evening when—for a few fleeting moments—the dwindling light becomes surreal. There is an eerie brightness that exists within the encroaching dark, like the world is torn in two. Those moments make me feel wildly exhilarated and like I'm going mad, all at once. The whole scene seemed so unreal, as if all of us were characters, all reading from scripts of who we believed we were supposed to be. I locked onto Tom 2's eyes in an effort to ground myself. "Weird that you never said what you thought of the story. The Salinger story."

"One of the greatest," he said, flicking his cigarette butt into the distance. "What about that beer?"

"Hey, thanks," I said. "I was actually thinking I'd swim against the tide and demonstrate my radical side by *not* having any beer this evening."

Tom 2 turned his back and went off into the dusk in search of a keg that had any remaining contents. "I get it," I said. "Man. Of. Few. Words."

Tom 1 laughed. Tom the original; Tommy from hereon. A beautiful, genuine, head-tossed-back, open-mouthed laugh. They passed one another, side by side for a moment, the two guys named Tom. They both had curly hair, but all similarity ended there. Tommy not only had an infectious and unfettered laugh but a huge, ready smile as well. He was tall and rangy and slightly uncomfortable in his own body, like a growing puppy. It made sense that he was the one person, of everyone I had met thus far, who had called out to me. Tommy was putting himself out there, casting his energy like it was so much fishing line, seeing where the hook might land. And he trusted that it would land somewhere good.

Cigarette Tom was compact and muscly. Dark brown hair, even darker eyes, deeply tanned skin. He was turned entirely inward, intense energy coiled over and under itself, swirling around and around. It seemed an effort for him to rouse himself from his own internal workings enough to form words, more effort to get the sounds to emerge from his mouth. And once he had made the effort, the sound of his own voice tormented him.

I loved them both. Immediately.

"Seriously," I said to Tommy as Tom went off to fetch more beer. "I'm kinda not used to this much drinking. Where I come from…I mean…I thought drinking was one of the things that we—our generation—really looked down on. Along with all the stuff our parents did that got us and the world into this crap state. All the hallmarks of the Establishment. I thought we rejected all that. Right?"

Tommy stared into his red cup, then took a long swig while an uncomfortable silence crept through the gathering. "Yeah. Not where I come from, my new friend. Hey, let me introduce you around, Esmé. This is my roommate Dave." Tommy gestured to one of the guys who lounged at his feet. "He's a genius. Certified. IQ 148."

Oh, my God, I thought. Is that an actual phrase? I've heard those *exact* words before! *Certified genius.* I had gone on only one college visit, which had been one visit more than I expected. Mom said that I could pick the school where I thought I was most likely to get accepted and get a scholarship, and if it was close enough to visit without having to spend a night, we could go and take a look. Around the middle of my junior year, Mom and I entered into an unspoken agreement that we would both essentially pretend that there was no such thing as college and no possibility that I would graduate high school and go to such an imaginary place. There wasn't a whole lot of discussion.

I planned the entire thing, in plenty of time for Mom to arrange the day off of work. We had to get up at the crack of dawn to make the three-hour drive and arrive in time for the 10:00 AM tour. Woozy with sleep, we drove mostly in silence, taking turns twisting the radio dial back and forth in an effort to find a local station with a reasonable absence of static.

I have no idea what it was about me, or how that had translated onto a college application, that said to the folks at the state university, "Let's pair Esmé with the engineers!" After the official meetings and tours and sample classes were finished, I was supposed to head off to one of the dorms for a slice of authentic college life—in this case, having dinner in the cafeteria and hanging around afterward with a group of freshman engineering students who lived on the same floor of a large dormitory. When I located the group of students who awaited me in the cafeteria, even on first glance, it seemed as if they must have been sent by a casting agency. A more universally pale, socially awkward, tic-laden, mismatched-plaid-wearing group of young men (and one virtually silent woman) could not possibly have come together without someone pulling the strings.

I loved them. I loved them, and I ached for them. I wished that they could stay on the same floor of that dorm for the rest of their lives, because I thought they had something very, very special that they would never have again, not once they left their mutual companionship behind. They would never have a community of other people who *got* them—who accepted their quirks unconditionally and who spoke their language. It made me want to adopt them and protect them from the future pain the world might inflict. But because I knew it was completely unrealistic for a seventeen-year-old to adopt a group of engineering students, I wished for them to stay right where they were. I settled for spending a few hours playing a highly odd game with the one guy who everyone referred to as the "certified genius." We moved little pieces of purple plastic back and forth on a palm-sized triangular playing board. I had absolutely no idea what was going on with that game, but the magnitude of Ken's delight at having a willing partner —well, it seemed like the very least I could do. You don't see that kind of unbridled joy every day, even if the bearer of that joy had never worn a pair of matching socks in his life.

Dave—the new would-be "certified genius" who stared at his fingers while he twiddled them around in various arrangements—tilted his chin very slightly, made a nanosecond of eye contact, and uttered a barely audible "Hey" while neither opening his mouth nor moving his lips.

"Hey, Dave," I said back. Giving him the once-over, I had no trouble believing that he may well be a genius. I just wasn't sure what that meant, in the real world, I mean.

Dave somehow looked as if he would have fit right in with the engineers, though they had been—within the limits of their own world—loud and gregarious and very friendly to me. A lot of their friendliness lay in the range of unselfconsciously batting around math jokes at one another. Dave looked as if he had never been comfortable anywhere, at any time. He radiated the effort being used to appear casual. He was doing his very best to appear as normal as he could.

Also, Dave was wearing a polo shirt. I had never seen a person my own age wearing a polo shirt in Clarion. Well, except for Danny, the kid who lived across the street diagonally from Mom and me. Every so often, his rich grandpa would take him out to dinner at the grandpa's country club. I didn't have much of an idea what a country club was, but all of us neighborhood kids had a highly unfavorable impression. Danny would have to break off from the neighborhood scene when his mother called him. A while later, he'd come back out with his strawberry blond hair neatly combed and plastered to his scalp. He'd have on a bright white polo shirt that emanated the pungent smell of bleach. Worst of all, he'd had to trade in his worn and beloved sneakers for a pair of highly polished penny loafers. We'd all stand around with him while he waited for his grandpa to pick him up and take him to dinner at the club.

We kept a respectable distance—bouncing our balls, strad-dling our bikes, kicking little pebbles—while Danny stood stock still for fear of getting a single speck of dirt on himself. We felt deep solidarity with his misery for being forced to give up a beautiful summer day, but more, for being forced to be someone different than the Danny that we knew.

Tommy continued around the circle making introductions. I decided to pre-empt the possibility of tanked-up frosh tee-tering to a standing position and shaking my hand like Tom had by saying, "Hey, really, don't get up. No need."

"This is Pauly," Tommy said. "Over there is Ben. The tall guy is Rob."

I looked at each of the three as Tommy introduced them. Pauly had a most distinctive way of taking a drag from his cig-arette—a deep draw followed by a dramatically quick with-drawal of the butt and a turn of his head. Ben had a weird little sneering smile. Rob gave me a wave then ran the fingers of his hand through his sandy blond hair a few times. I found Pauly and Rob adorable. And Ben, an arrogant sourpuss.

"And right here is Natalie. She's from Texas," Tommy con-tinued.

I had no idea why Tommy singled out the Texas informa-tion, or what I was supposed to do with it. I waved kind of lamely at everyone and said, "Hi, all." I turned to Natalie. "Yeah…Texas. Cool accent, I'm guessing."

Natalie laughed and said, "Well, I'm thinkin' it pegs me pretty quick as not being from around here." She was right. Her drawl was leisurely and thick, to such a degree that it seemed a shade deliberate. Natalie had very long, disturbingly unhealthy hair. She had a tiny frame with exceptionally long legs and big boobs that she seemed intent on displaying, as her polo shirt was a good couple of sizes too small. Wait. Polo shirt, again.

"Oh," Tommy said, "Oh, God, I'm so sorry. This is Adele."

I felt like an awful person for taking one look at Adele and understanding completely why Tommy would have forgotten about her. She had a tiny little frame, in that baby-bird way that can be hard to look at without feeling slightly squeamish about the translucent skin and evident vulnerability. Adele's hair and facial features appeared to be all one color. She seemed to blend into the background so much that I had a difficult time focusing on her. I thought that this was probably the story of her life—not being noticed, not significant-seeming enough to be overlooked because she hadn't been seen in the first place. It made me want to like her, to hope that I would. "Adele!" I said. "Cool. Another unusual name. I've only known one other Adele in my life. She was the piano teacher for my ballet class when I was a kid. She was a riot."

"Yeah, it's not a very common name," Adele said. I felt an enormous sense of relief that I was able to overcome my initial inclination to laugh when I heard Adele's voice. High-pitched, squeaky, nasal in a way that seemed to go straight from her mouth to that spot on your forehead, right between your eyes. Instant headache.

"Adele the pianist chain smoked the entire time she was playing ballet pieces for us little girls. The ashtray on the edge of her keyboard would be *filled* by the end of an hour-long class. Her voice was so low, and so raspy-hoarse that I'm pretty sure she must have been hitting the whiskey pretty hard, too." I pantomimed like I was taking slugs from a bottle.

I was trying too hard. Way too hard. I probably had been for a while, certainly since that idiotic remark about "showing my radical side." No, before that, even. I was some exaggerated version of myself. Aggressively rebellious, or something. Thank God it had gotten too dark for anyone to see me blushing. I could feel the heat in my cheeks. The pulsing at my temples.

I did this thing sometimes where I sort of turned off the sound. I stopped listening—just for a minute—to what people were saying. I shut out the words. I watched them then, their gestures and their movements. With the sound track off, I could see different things. I saw that everyone was trying too hard. Every person sitting around in this random little group collected by the super-extroverted Tommy on our third full day of our first year at college.

We had a clean slate. We were all brand-new. Each of us understood this in our own way, and the knowledge was at once thrilling and terrifying. We had no idea, none whatsoever, what we were meant to do. We introduced ourselves to other brand-new people who knew nothing about who we were before we arrived here. Whether we were the one who spent every Saturday night in the bathroom, leaning into the mirror as we squeezed the zits under the harsh lights. Whether we were the one who left behind a sweet and tender first love full of breathy whispers and dreamy sighs. Whether we were the one whose parents travelled the world and left us completely alone while we rode a unicycle through the maze of our hallways. Whatever we had been, whatever triumphs and suffering lay behind us, we began anew.

When I saw Tom approaching the group with his newly full beer, I turned the sound back on. In my head. He slowed, but didn't stop walking. "I'm turning in for the night," he said. "Just swung by to say goodnight."

"Prefer to be by yourself when you drink alone?" I said to his receding back.

"Squalor," Tom said, without turning. "I'm extremely interested in squalor."

CHAPTER 12

I HAD BEEN TO ALL OF MY OTHER CLASSES—A COUPLE OF them more than once—before my special English program met for its three-hour allotment on Wednesday night. The first time the ten of us convened, I felt like I was back in grade school. That anxious/excited butterfly tummy feeling of walking through the doorway on the first day of school, into the room where you'd be for the whole upcoming year. Subtly taking inventory of the kids who were already there and seated. Oh, look, Bonnie and Cindy are here. Cool. No, no, not Karen again. I can't do Karen again. And you know that every single one of those kids is looking right at you, and they're all thinking their own judging thoughts. Then you watch every new kid who walks through the door, and you size them up, and you store it all away, trying to get some initial bearings, some sense of the year that stretches so far ahead.

All ten of us had arrived and were nervously/expectantly making skimpy introductions and awkward chit chat when Dr. David Ackerman made his entrance. He blew into the room, took off his sports coat, rolled up his sleeves, told us to call him David, and plopped a gallon jug of Taylor Cream

Sherry onto the table, complete with a stack of plastic glasses balanced precariously on the bottle's neck. All eyes locked onto the bottle. "David" implored us to go ahead and pour ourselves some sherry while he organized his papers and notes and such. When no one moved, he reached over and twisted off the screw cap by way of encouragement.

A gallon of sherry in a glass jug is mighty heavy. I had to stand up to pour myself a glass, but I did not hesitate to do so. The few minutes of jittery small talk and the dramatic entrance of David Ackerman were all the impetus I needed to conclude that a stiff drink, if Taylor Cream Sherry could be considered a stiff drink, was most certainly called for. The only real drinking I had done in high school was the occasional grain alcohol punch at parties where the main focus was entirely on the *other* substances being consumed. No one drank grain alcohol punch for the flavor; the various additives that comprised the "punch" were an all-out effort to *disguise* any alcohol flavor that might break through. It had already become abundantly clear that my high school near-sobriety would be going by the wayside with the starring role that alcohol played at this college, and a hefty pour of cream sherry during this class seemed an excellent place to start.

My first sip of the sherry coincided with my fellow student Anna covering her mouth to giggle while she poured her own drink, then she repeated the giggle gesture while she raised the cup to her mouth. Unaccustomed to drinking as I was at that early point in the year, by Anna's second giggle, I lamented that I had not poured a much larger amount into my cup the first time around and would undoubtedly be the first person diving in for a second round.

I stared at each of my nine fellow students as we went around the table making our formal introductions. Each person said where they were from, detailed their reasons for having applied to this program, and listed their goals for the year. I thought if I stared hard enough, well enough, deeply enough, I might locate something, a possibility, a slender thread of chance for a real friend among the nine Early Concentration in English students who would sit around this table with me until May.

Henry from Berkeley, who was dressed almost identically to Dr. David Ackerman and said that he did hope to be an English professor himself one day. Terry from Long Island, still plagued by a stubborn case of acne but a thoroughly disarming, gap-toothed smile. Keith from Hawaii, who had found and formed a friendship with Vic from Syracuse. They already seemed inseparable and, sadly, indistinguishable in their eager blandness. The aforementioned Anna, who showed an appealing goofy side behind the giggles. A kid whose name I didn't quite catch who was so painfully shy and awkward and self-conscious and anxious and twitchy that I could feel myself squirming in my seat. I took an extra-large swig of sherry from my glass on his behalf, and I stopped paying such close attention to the remaining three people because it had become physically painful by that point.

I did not see the thread that I was looking for, the slender and tentative sign of hope that one of these nine people might have had something in their own brief history that could resonate with my own.

My soul took a bit of a dip.

It was funny how the jug of sherry had seemed comical in its outsized bulk at the beginning of class. It didn't seem that way anymore.

CHAPTER 13

THE SAME MINDS THAT HAD COLLECTIVELY CONCEIVED OF housing the entire freshman class on its own separate campus extended that idea to having all one thousand of us eat in our own separate dining hall. One thousand of us waiting in multiple lines to jockey for one thousand chairs placed in a room roughly the size of an emptied-out warehouse. Just as I knew I would be planning my days around minimizing trips up and down the five flights of stairs to my dorm room, I quickly realized that getting back in line *again* for seconds on food needed to be avoided at all costs. You'd better get everything you needed the first time around. Looking at the trays of my fellow diners, other people had figured this out as well. Most of the guys whose trays I scanned had comically heaped up dinner plates, two or three desserts and several full glasses of milk. We weren't especially adventurous eaters in Clarion, Pennsylvania, and I was highly skeptical about any of the cooked dishes that had been mass produced for a thousand of us. It had taken me years to convince my mother to let me pack my own school lunches, starting in junior high. It was a tough sell, too, because we qualified for the school's hot lunches for free, thanks to Harry S. Truman and the National

School Lunch Act. I had never gotten over my little kid fear of tiny old women in hairnets, serving up plates from enormous steaming cauldrons. Consequently, I stuck with a giant salad, a carton of yogurt—things it seemed safe to assume would be edible—and four cups of coffee. I couldn't fit five on my tray.

"Are you like her at all?"

"Would it kill you to talk in complete sentences, with complete thoughts that others could actually follow?" I said to Tom. He had come over to where I sat alone at a dining table in the massive dining hall and set his tray down. Yet he remained standing behind the chair in front of him, as if his final decision about whether to sit rested on my answer to his question.

" 'I purely came over because I thought you looked extremely lonely,' " he said.

"Oh, my lord," I said. "Do you seriously have the entire Salinger story memorized? The whole thing? It seems like you do." I laughed when I said it, but I looked at him a little more closely. Emily Dickenson's poem flashed through my thoughts: *I'm Nobody. Who are you? Are you—Nobody—too?*

"Nah," he said.

"It's weird. Kids our age generally don't know that story, let alone have chunks of it committed to memory."

He shrugged, pulled out the chair and sat down.

"Are you a Salinger fanatic or something?" I asked him.

"Nah," he said. "I wouldn't say so."

"I still think it's pretty unusual. Seems like someone who's got such a close relationship with a lesser-known J.D. Salinger story is the kind of person who would be in my English seminar thing. It's a whole collection of highly odd people, my-self included. Not in an awful way, really."

"It's not lesser-known. It's considered one of the best short stories ever written. Also, one of the best works of short fiction about World War II. Ever. I mean, shell shock. He brought shell shock to light," Tom said. "In a short work, I mean. Shorter than say, *All Quiet on the Western Front.* And published in *The New Yorker.* Entirely different readership reached. Anyway, not 'lesser-known.'"

There seemed to be a chasm between the passion and interest that Tom's words suggested and the utterly expressionless, deadpan delivery of those words. I didn't know what to say.

Tom took a salt shaker from his jacket pocket and proceeded to pour an ungodly amount of salt across every single thing on his plate.

"It would save time if you just took the top off," I said.

"You didn't answer the question," Tom said.

"What question?"

"Are you anything like her?"

"Like who?" I asked.

He cocked an eyebrow and stared at me.

"I'm wondering if I might be able to get actual college credit for this. Deciphering the subtle cues and clues of Tom…hey, what's your last name?"

"Donahue," he said.

"Deciphering the secret language of Tom Donahue, 101."

"You're witty, then," he said.

"Please notice that I have four cups of coffee on my tray,

whereas you have three glasses of milk," I said. "Which means that I am intensely caffeinated and have not forgotten your question. I think you are asking me if I am anything like Esmé, the character in the story Esmé, at least, that's what I think you meant."

Tom winked at me while shoveling forkfuls of differently flavored salt into his mouth.

"I have a decent vocabulary," I said. "Otherwise, you'll have to decide for yourself."

"You're precocious like the character—if you don't mind me saying," Tom said.

"I believe I'm too old to be precocious," I said. "Isn't that term reserved for the very young? Now I'm just, I don't know, old before my time, or something like that. Hopefully not quite a burn-out. Not just yet." I'm sure it was entirely evident that this was meant to be light-hearted banter, well within the realm of cafeteria conversation befitting two people who barely knew one another.

"I think Salinger's insight was that when people are so unusually mature, it's because they've suffered. Suffered intensely. Great loss, and all that."

"I've never seen anyone put so much salt on their food. Not to mention that you carry your own salt shaker. If twenty-four hours goes by and you still haven't peed, I think that's your signal that you need to cut back." Yes, it was a blatant, unsubtle, and wholly clumsy change of subject on my part. But he had crossed a line. Much as I longed for a Nobody, it was way too soon to step into quicksand.

CHAPTER 14

It was a strange thing about Clarion, Pennsylvania, that many of the kids I grew up with seemed *old,* as if they must be very small, middle-aged people trapped inside young, gangly bodies. Debbie Applebaum with her paper-thin cardigans and severe bangs. Elaine Peloski with her pointy-framed glasses and persistent expression of mild disdain. My friend Pattianne called it "the stinky cheese face." Valerie Seagram with her sad slouch that made her seem utterly beaten down by life at the age of ten.

They were waiting, biding their time, stuck inside childhoods that made no sense to them. They gamely skipped rope. They teetered on one leg as they bent down to toss their pebbles on the hopscotch board. They did all of the normal things, but it looked all wrong.

As my fourth-grade class trudged up the staircase in single-file lockstep, Debbie Applebaum put her thin, dry fingers on my arm, leaned in close, and whispered in my ear, "Bruce Baker *smells!* Have you noticed?"

She immediately snapped back upright into model staircase-climbing decorum so she wouldn't get caught talking in line. I didn't have to answer. I don't believe she got a glimpse of the stunned expression on my face, either. But I got a good look at hers, and the look of utter scornful condemnation rattled me. In so young a person, such chilly disdain stabbed at my heart.

There wasn't any particular wisdom that went with this tendency toward premature agedness. It was not as if these children were sage old souls in a way that would have been lovely. It was like they had come into the world with their attitudes and opinions and tastes fully formed. Genetically imprinted or otherwise predetermined, they would not need to go through all the bothersome life experiences along the road to forming the array of attributes that make us who we are. Every time I looked at Debbie Applebaum, I pictured her wearing a starched apron and dabbing at distasteful smudges and smears on the faces of her abashed kids. Elaine Peloski would spend every spare moment organizing her cupboards and cabinets and drawers into precise, orderly arrangements. A cigarette would dangle precariously from Valerie Seagram's mouth while she held a baby on one hip, stirred a pot on the stove, and yelled half-heartedly at her other kids without ever turning around to look at them. A stray ash would make its way into the family's dinner, and Valerie would not care.

Whereas my Clarion agemates seemed to have all their ideas and opinions cemented into immovable places, it was as if a lot of my classmates at my new college had merely dressed for the part. All shine and no substance. Meaning that they had that same quality of seeming to be squarely ensconced in middle age, but without the staunch and unwavering opinions. Without opinions at all, really. Or ideas. It was like they were waiting to be told what to think, at some point in the future. In the meantime, their lives were largely about checking off boxes.

Case in point: Montgomery Treadwell III.

Montgomery, who didn't have a nickname and never had, lived one floor below Tom and two floors below Tommy. The same staircase led to all of their rooms, so I saw a great deal of Montgomery Treadwell III that fall. Coming out of his room to fetch his copy of the *Wall Street Journal.* Coming out of his room to grab the freshly polished penny loafers he'd left in the entryway so his room wouldn't smell of shoeshine. Coming out of his room in a fancy polo shirt while the weather was still hot, then a fancy starched button-down shirt when it finally got a little cooler, then with a fancy sweater draped over his shoulders and tied across his chest when the mornings got cooler still.

I tried. I swear I did.

We both did.

"Hey, Montgomery," I said as I encountered him approximately 215 times a week. "How's it going?"

"I'm well, Esmé. You?" Montgomery would say.

I did my best to ignore the fact that he always said, "I'm well," which was just not how regular people talked, and to also ignore the fact that he was always dressed like he was ready to run off to The Club for a round of golf and a couple of stiff drinks to seal some deal where massive fortunes would be made by people who already possessed massive fortunes. "Doing OK," I would say. "Except for my Logic class. Which is seriously trying to kill me. I'm not sure what I was thinking, signing up for that one."

"You never know how it might come in handy later," he would say.

"Yeah, sometimes you do know. I feel pretty confident in saying that I don't expect to stumble upon a future use for this stuff. Ever."

Montgomery chuckled in a good-natured way. "You have such strong opinions about things."

I refrained from saying, "I'm not sure they're all that strong. I think you're not used to opinions, maybe." Instead, I said, "Hey, what do you read in the *Wall Street Journal?* I've never known anyone who read it."

"That can't possibly be true," he said, chuckling, still in what seemed to be his characteristic affable way, but with a bit of wariness creeping in.

"Yeah. Pretty sure," I said. "But, you know, I'm from small-town Pennsylvania and all."

"It's just what everybody reads," he said, in a tone that suggested he believed he had given a comprehensive answer.

"Uh, huh," I said, in a tone that suggested that wasn't an answer at all. He looked at me with a degree of genuine bewilderment. He looked, in fact, like he might be edging toward disorientation.

"I read it. Every day. All of it."

It seemed as if he may have started to feel upset, and I felt bad. "Hey, just asking. Nice sweater, by the way. Great color on you."

Montgomery beamed and said "Thanks." He had regained his balance, and I continued up the stairs to collect one or both of the Tommy Twins.

Of course, we didn't have that one particular conversation over and over. But my attempts to engage in a little friendly small talk invariably went in that general direction. Like when I encountered him picking up his loafers from their place outside his door, and I said, "Wow, I don't think I've polished a pair of shoes since I was about six years old. I used to *love* covering up the scuff marks on my saddle shoes with white polish. I went nuts with that stuff!" I got the same, "That can't possibly be true" response. I got that a lot. As if my whole life utterly baffled him, this young woman from Pennsylvania who had independently formed opinions, did not read the *WSJ*, did not polish her shoes, and seemed to be interested in forming substantive friendships with two men who lived upstairs from him, relationships which did not appear to be romantic in nature.

And whereas all of this is, in fact, truth, it is also, of course, a metaphor.

Meaning that there were a lot of people very much like Montgomery Treadwell III. There were a lot of *Wall Street Journals* outside a lot of dormitory rooms every morning. Kids my age opened their doors to fetch their *WSJs* wearing pajamas that looked as if they'd be *ironed,* covered by plush monogrammed bathrobes, their feet toasty in sheepskin scuffs. I slept in old, ripped T-shirts from various rock concerts that comprised the high points of my high school life, and a pair of undies.

My "slippers" were a pair of flip flops purchased from the drug store, and the robe I threw on to walk down the hall to the bathroom was the one my mother had made me several years earlier. The original rose color had morphed and faded into a truly disgusting shade of pink. Threads had pulled lose from the terry cloth in a million places and hung like worn out tinsel from a Christmas tree. The entire collar was gradually turning itself inside out, and I could not even imagine giving up this robe—ever—for a new one.

Montgomery came out of his room one morning looking particularly linksman-like, even for him, and I couldn't help myself. I said, "Jesus, Montgomery, are you planning on nine holes today or eighteen?"

He laughed aloud and said, "As if there's a decent course anywhere near here. There's not, as I'm sure you know."

"Yeah, right," I said. "Of course. Everyone knows that." I had already passed his doorway and started up the next set of stairs because I'd thought Montgomery was being cleverly ironic and we had, therefore, enjoyed a brief, witty, entirely successful morning encounter. Then the truth hit me, and his comment stopped me in my tracks. "So, you actually play golf, then? You don't just really like the clothes?"

"Of course, I play. Don't tell me you've never been on a golf course."

"Of course, I've been on a golf course!" I countered. "One of my absolute favorite places in the world to get high. Usually Clarion Oaks, but if someone was willing to do the drive, Pinecrest was a vastly superior place to get wasted. Plus, Pinecrest had their self-proclaimed world-famous homemade potato chips, and oh my God, they really were insanely good, I have to say, though I never actually had them when I wasn't completely blazed, and nothing beat the challenge of walking into the snack shop completely ripped and trying to purchase some salty greasy crunchy amazing chips. One time my friend Joe started eating them right away, right in the shop while I was still trying to manage the whole concept of counting and exchanging money for material goods. Joe was grabbing giant handfuls of the chips and sort of crushing them into his mouth—one right after the other like a film that's been sped up or something—and when I'd finished paying and putting away the change, I looked over at him and his entire body from the bottom of his nose down to his waist was completely covered in little teeny tiny crushed up potato chips. Completely. Covered. I seriously thought they were going to call security, that's how hard I was laughing. Have I ever been on a golf course?"

It was a great memory, and I was transported into a reverie that was so deep and so poignant that it was very nearly unbearable—until I saw the expression on Montgomery's face. He was looking at me as if I were from Mars. "Montgomery," I said, "I think maybe I was going to loud concerts and even louder protests and wearing bell bottoms and handing out love beads and drawing peace signs everywhere and sneaking a hit or two of pot every chance I got while you were playing golf."

I said it not with rancor, but rather with pain. There we stood,

Montgomery Treadwell III and I, not ten feet between the two of us in actual distance, but a universe between the two of us in every other way. A universe that could not be bridged, even by two eighteen-year-old kids who had the world open in front of us, even with both of us wishing to bridge that distance, and both of us trying.

And we both knew this.

CHAPTER 15

WE WERE SQUIRRELS THAT FALL. THAT'S HOW I THOUGHT about it. All of us: squirrels with the winter approaching. There was a peculiar, urgent energy that ran beneath the surface of our lives. Even those of us who attacked all-out partying with a vengeance. Even those of us who holed up in tiny little study cubicles in the library night and day. It was like we all had the same sickness that we were all pretending we didn't have. "No, I don't have a cold. My nose always runs with thick green goo at this time of year! Strange, isn't it?" "Yeah, I don't have a cold either. I have to remember to let my coffee cool down before I drink it; that's why my throat is killing me!"

Squirrel, squirrel. We hid our bewilderment, pretended it was nothing but *amazing* to be away from home. We swept our insecurities into the corners and under the carpet as best we could, acting as if living and communing with total strangers who were continually assessing us did not make us one bit uncomfortable. And no, we were not especially disconcerted by having been thrust into quasi-adulthood; we were completely accustomed to getting ourselves up, making it to our classes on time, handling a full academic load with no supervision or help or support or hand-holding, managing our food and laundry and finances without spending every last penny we'd been allotted within the first week once we learned that every bar in the area would serve us, no questions asked. Most importantly, we were absolutely not see-sawing wildly between glee and terror at the scope of our newfound freedom.

We were *not* disoriented! How could we have been after that solid week of careful, thorough orientation on the school's part?

Squirrel, squirrel.

The strain was ever-present, the tinge of pressure. We scurried to gather up our cache of nuts. I envisioned each of us freshmen sitting cross-legged on the quad's sea of grass. In front of each person lay a huge pile—our acorns—which represented the pieces of our lives. The mission at hand was to figure out exactly what to *do* with our pile. Every decision about every acorn mattered.

Except, it wasn't actually *all* of us, I noticed. There were kids here and there who didn't seem to have the sickness. I couldn't figure it out, and it niggled at me. At first, I thought it was the kids who had spent long periods of time away from home well before they arrived at college—they had summered on the Continent, or polished their dressage at equestrian camps, and the like. But there were lots of squirrels who had, in fact, spent most of the previous four *years* away from home, as a large number of the freshman class had sauntered off to boarding schools all over the world, and many of them were still plenty squirrelly.

That's when I learned to understand the distinction between the truly wealthy and the merely rich. For the most part, it was the wealthy kids who were not squirrels.

But I still did not understand *why*.

They sat with their puzzle pieces just like we all did. They spent the same amount of time arranging their acorns. They exerted the same degree of focus and energy at the task before them. Still, something was missing. It was as if…they'd showed up at the track, they'd placed their bets, they'd polished the lenses of their binoculars to a pristine gleam to get the best possible view, yet they acted like they didn't have a horse in the race. No real stake.

I recalled the infamous, memorable, quotable, viciously bitter passage from F. Scott Fitzgerald, "Let me tell you about the very rich. They are different from you and me." Ernest Hemingway supposedly quipped back, "Yes, they have more money," which is an outstanding response and a good yarn; it would have been an excellent addition to the annals of exchanges between the two titans of literature over the course of their long, complicated friendship. But it never happened. I looked it up in the library.

The library. So many of my fellow frosh could not get enough of the school's library. Many were inclined to wander into rhapsody at the drop of a hat over the tower! The reading rooms!! The stained glass, the murals, the eighty solid miles of shelf space!!! I, on the other hand, strove to avoid the library to the furthest extent possible. Don't get me wrong. *Actual* Gothic cathedrals—with their five defining features: stained glass, pointed arches, ribbed vaults, *flying buttresses* (as excellent a design concept and phrase as has ever been invented!), and various ornate embellishments that might include such things as gargoyles and other hideous creatures that doubled as water spouts! Amazing! (History of Architecture and Art 101 did include some truly great stuff, as it turned out)— stood among the most stunning human creations on earth. I dreamed of the day I might get to see them, structures that I imagined would have their rich history suffused into every stone and nook and cranny. Even the thought of such wonder was dizzying. On the other hand, a structure built in 1931 as a *replica* seemed like Velveeta, or cheese in a can, next to a fine aged cheddar. It depressed me to think about, let alone go inside the fake Gothic construction. The fact that I ventured into the library *voluntarily* marked the depth of my sincerity —some might say obsession—with trying to comprehend the whole enigma about the students who were not squirrels.

CHAPTER 16

BY THE BEGINNING OF OCTOBER, I HAD GOTTEN INTO THE
habit of knocking on Tom Donahue's door at any old time of
the day that I wasn't doing much else. Maybe it was because
it was one less flight of stairs than it would have been to Tommy's room. Maybe it was because of Tom's roommate Mark.
Maybe it was for other reasons entirely. I certainly felt a pull,
a tug, in Tom's direction, an itchy curiosity that stopped me
at his door. It had nothing to do with the extra flight of stairs
to Tommy's room, really.

Tom and Mark had lucked into the same situation that my
roommate Carrie and I had—two people in a suite that had
been designed for three. Almost as much room as I had growing up with Mom. Well, not really; but each person had their
own bedroom, and there was a decent-sized living room to
use for whatever you wanted as well.

If Tom wasn't in his room, Mark would shout—if such a soft
voice could be considered shouting, "Come on in." I would
invariably find Mark in his bedroom, sitting on his bed with
his legs stretched out and his ankles crossed, reading a book.
He would turn the book upside down, place the book in his
lap and say, "Hi, Esmé. Tom isn't here."

"Right. I noticed that," I would say. "I came in because I was actually wondering how *you're* doing."

He had an enigmatic, Mona Lisa smile. "Good," he would say. "Things are good."

"Good. Glad to hear it. Hey, tell Tom I stopped by. Just wanted to see how you were doing."

"You can wait, if you want," Mark would say.

"I didn't bring anything with me. To do. I'll catch up with Tom later."

"You can wait with me. Talk, if you want," Mark would say. "I have some time."

I'm not sure if I had the same conversations with people over and over before I went to college, or not. Maybe this phenomenon hadn't happened before; maybe I wasn't aware of it before. But, as with Montgomery Treadwell III, Mark and I did that same verbal dance many, many times.

Mark completely fascinated me, much like a visitor from another planet might fascinate me. Everything about him seemed freshly *pressed,* like he had just finished ironing his entire *being* moments before I arrived. It never ceased to amaze me that—as far as I could tell—he did all of his schoolwork from that same position on his bed. And yet there was nary a wrinkle on his sheets, his blanket, his pillow. Same with the entirety of his clothing. Not a crease nor a fold *anywhere.*

I learned a fair amount about him over the course of the fall. He had grown up in the city of San Francisco, a fact that struck me as wildly exotic in every way. His parents owned a small neighborhood grocery store, and he was their only child. Their store and their home were close together in a part of the city near the ocean, and Mark had been free to wander between the two locations from an early age. Mark said it was foggy in that area of the city all the time, that there were fewer than a handful of truly sunny days each *year*. I found this very hard to believe and thought he must be pulling my leg, except that it was Mark—not a person who would ever, under any circumstances, pull anyone's leg. I envisioned a childhood surrounded by luscious fruits and sumptuous vegetables and tidy stacks of pantry items all ensnared in a dense, unremitting fog.

"Were you lonely?" I asked him one day.

He gave me that Mona Lisa smile and said nothing, so I continued. "Everything you say about growing up, it all seems so...shrouded. Not just by the fog. You describe it like you were so alone. So, I wonder. Were you lonely?"

"Why do you ask?"

"Because I want to know." I said, "I want to know *you*."

"I don't really trust you, Esmé," Mark said.

I was shocked. "What do you mean?" I asked him. "Why not?"

"I don't know how anyone can be so good-natured all the time, so interested in everyone, so...*happy*. I'm just not sure that's trustworthy."

Do I really have them fooled? I thought. All of them? Fooled.

CHAPTER 17

ONE GLANCE THROUGH MY WINDOW ON THAT MID-OCTOBER morning and a surge of mixed-up feelings welled within me. I put the palm of my hand against the windowpane to confirm my hunch, and I felt the sun-touched warmth that, sure enough, reached all the way through the glass. Indian summer. One of those unexpected days that come after a string of dreary, damp autumn days that chill your entire soul, and suddenly, a warm, sunny day that could pass for the height of summer save for the fuller, more saturated gold of the sun's light. The leaves had barely begun to change color, trees looking as if they had been delicately dabbed by a divine paintbrush.

Indian summer in Clarion—with the ripe sun falling across the expanse of wooded hills and the barest aromas of leaves and apples tinging the warm air—comprised some of my most treasured memories of perfect days on earth. Apple picking with Mom. Long walks through the woods, alone, immersed in a sea of towering trees, bird songs, and the crunch of leaves under my feet. Fresh apple cider at roadside stands. The first morning that frost coated each individual blade of grass.

The ache was so powerful it felt like a hand had reached into me and grabbed my guts and squeezed them. I missed my mom and my hometown so much in that moment that I wanted to start running and not stop until I reached Pennsylvania. If I couldn't throw my arms around my mother and wander around Cook Forest State Park, and walk across the teetering swinging bridge, and listen to the wind making that low whistling sound when it swirled through the hemlocks....

I had yet to locate any firm sense of what I was doing at this school, so far away from everything I had known, so filled with peers who felt as if they had come from entirely different worlds. I had felt these things every day, but on a day such as this....

All the wretched misery of loneliness and homesickness that I didn't even know had been burbling around unnoticed suddenly hurtled to the surface. I needed to talk to her. If I could not see my mother right in front of me, I needed to hear her voice. I knew she would be at work. Mom always worked on Saturday mornings, because Dr. McClelland always worked on Saturday mornings—9:00 AM until noon, as long as I could remember. And I knew she had told me to never, ever call her at work unless it was a genuine emergency of the life-hanging-on-by-a-thread type. It was 11:15, and I knew that there were only forty-five more minutes until it would be all right to call, but it didn't matter. I couldn't wait. I dialed the number that had been branded into my brain since I was five years old, and she picked up after the second ring. "Dr. McClelland's office, may I help you?" my mother said in the same efficient, professional, friendly but not too, cheery but not too, tone she had managed to duplicate without variation for the thirteen years she had spent in his office. I could picture her gracefully crossed ankles. Sometimes I was convinced that the only time she had ever uncrossed those ankles was when my dad and she conceived me.

"Mom," I said.

"What's wrong? Tell me what's happened," she said.

"Nothing, I'm fine. I—"

"Esmé!" my mother said in a seething whisper that immediately indicted my unspeakable mistake in having the immaturity and poor judgment to call during working hours.

Her tone instantly sobered me with a weighty guilt. "I'm sorry. I should never have called when you're working."

My tone instantly sobered her with the weight of maternal guilt. "No, no. I'm sure you have a good reason," she said.

"I don't, really," I said. "Just wanted to talk. Sorry again. Talk soon. Bye." I put the receiver back in the cradle feeling too sad to even cry. I needed to get outside. I needed to find a place where I could walk among lots and lots of trees on this staggeringly beautiful day and smell the unmistakable smell of leaves at the very beginning of their journey toward their own oblivion.

I dug through a stack of pamphlets and other handouts that we'd all been given way back during Orientation Week, remembering that there had been some maps and information about the surrounding area. Sure enough, I found the map I had vaguely remembered, which included two large green areas with a very few streets traversing them: North Cliffs Park and South Cliffs Park.

North Cliffs was slightly smaller, but it was also a bit closer. South Cliffs looked enormous from the amount of space it took up on the map, and it looked like it may be a more straightforward route to walk there. But it was definitely farther. It seemed like kind of a toss-up, but I ultimately settled on North Cliffs for its proximity. I shoved the map into the back pocket of my jeans and decided to swing by the weekend brunch. I wanted to grab a big cup of coffee and some food to eat along the way.

When I hit the bottommost landing of my staircase, one of the resident advisor Scandinavian clones popped out from her room. The willowy one. "Hey, Esmé. How's it going? Haven't seen you for a while."

I immediately felt like I had just been accused of something, but I had no idea what it might be. "Good, good," I said. "I'm good. Was figuring I'd walk to North Cliffs on this amazing day."

The other advisor came out of the room then. She stood partway behind the willowy one, sort of peering around her at me. Willowy said, "North Cliffs? No. Sorry. No. You can't walk there. It's not safe. To walk. It's really not." Not Willowy nodded slowly and mutely.

"Really?" I asked, looking from one to the other. "Oh, ok, well, good thing I brought the map with me. I'll walk to South Cliffs then."

Not Willowy had already started shaking her head back

and forth, and Willowy said, "Not safe. No way. You definitely can't walk *there.*"

"Really?" I couldn't believe it. "The two biggest parks in the area, early on a Saturday afternoon, and you're seriously saying that it's not safe to go to them? Either of them?"

"I'm sure there's gonna be a ton of kids hanging out on the lawns all over campus today. Plenty to do."

"Yeah, I bet you're right." I wasn't about to say that the very last thing I wanted was "a ton of kids." Teeming humanity —especially from this school—was the exact thing I needed respite from.

"Sorry, Esmé. We just really want you to stay safe," Willowy said while the clone nodded.

I told my advisors that I was going to grab some coffee before brunch closed down—mainly as an excuse to get away from the bland blonde safety-conscious spreaders of good cheer. A few steps outside, I stopped in the middle of the big old dorm's open terrace. I had no idea where I might go or what I might do. Maybe I'd head off to one of the Cliffs in spite of the clones' dire warnings of jeopardy and peril. Maybe I wouldn't. Anything I chose would be arbitrary, and would mostly be part of a sustained, all-out effort to not crumble. I stood in the full, glorious sunlight visualizing myself graying and molding and putrefying like a fallen leaf on the forest floor.

"Hey, Esmé! Big night last night?" Tommy. Ambling through the gate, apparently coming back from brunch judging by the Styrofoam cup in his hand. I thought about whether I had seen him with anything but a bright red solo cup. Ever.

"Nah," I said. "Just debating whether it's worth it to walk over to the dining hall for a cup of truly awful coffee."

"I thought it was always worth it to you. I've seen you with four or five cups on your *dinner* tray," Tommy said.

I was both charmed and annoyed by his bouncy Adam's apple and his winning, toothy smile. "Well, that's different. It has that special *je ne sais quoi* when it's been sitting around on the burner since breakfast. Sort of like eating used charcoal briquettes."

He laughed that laugh of his, and I wanted to simultaneously slap him and grab onto his wild curly hair so I could press my lips against his and insert my tongue between his gleaming teeth and probe deeply within the nether regions of his mouth. Life was a fucking mess.

"I gotta run. But I was going to call you before my study group and tell you about tonight."

"Study group on a Saturday afternoon? That is the kind of ambition and spirit that keeps the wheels turning. I'm very impressed. Also a bit frightened."

"I'm never sure whether you're being serious or sarcastic. Or do I mean ironic?"

"You sound like my mom," I said.

"Well, anyway. A bunch of us are going to a bar tonight. One that Rob found. It reminds him of the ones he loves in Chicago."

"Wow, no free alcohol on campus tonight? That would seriously surprise me."

"Fear not. I'm sure it's there to be had. We just thought this would be fun. I think Rob's homesick, a little."

I looked away. That one hit hard.

"I can spot you the cash, if you're short." The sweet boy had misinterpreted my expression. "I'd love to."

"No, no, I'm good. Caffeine deprived; that's all."

"Come with us tonight! If I don't see you at dinner, come on by around seven. We'll wait for you." He started walking toward his dorm and gave me the same big, full-armed wave that he'd hailed me with on the night of our first meeting.

CHAPTER 18

I WAS STARING INTO THE BOTTOM OF A MOSTLY EMPTY GLASS. Nothing but an alarmingly red maraschino cherry and ice dregs. Beautifully rounded ice dregs, though, their soft edges reflecting the dim blue ceiling lights of the bar in a truly dazzling rainbow display. The colorful scene felt aggressively satiric—the bruised fake leather of the booths in a color that had once been orange, the dark walnut of the peeling rec room paneling, the rays of blue light from the opaque glass that shrouded the lightbulbs, and the leering cherry at the bottom of my glass—as if everything in the room had been purposely exaggerated to poke fun at its own decrepit bad taste.

The problem was: I didn't like alcohol. Didn't like the taste of it. Didn't like the idea of it. Since this school and its student population seemed intent on promoting its merits, I had been trying to find an alcoholic beverage I could tolerate. I was working on whiskey sours right then, which is why I was staring at a maraschino cherry and thinking that the color alone should have told us that those things would kill you well before the red dye #whatever research came out. I'd already cycled through daiquiris. And vodka gimlets. The ever-present, ever-popular drink of all my new acquaintances—beer—

completely turned my stomach. My first whiskey sour had been unwretched enough that I thought I'd order a second.

It was the first time I'd seen the nondescript Adele since we were introduced the night I met the Tommy Twins, etc. She sat directly across from me, and Tommy sat beside me to my left. Rob and four or five other folks sat to the left of Adele and Tommy, making it pretty hard for me to talk to any of them. The bartender was such a pronounced "type," it seemed as if she must have auditioned for the part: aging beauty queen who hadn't lost her sparkle and managed to seem both world-weary and genuinely interested in every single thing that every single person said. She was terrific. She came over to our table and stood there with her hands on her hips and a wry, dimpled smile—the signal to order up quick and let her get back to the bar. Adele sat up straighter and said, "I'd like Sex on the Beach." Her courage faltered then, I guess, as she slumped back down and looked up through her bangs as she added, "Please?" and I decided right then to eat the cherry and take my chances on a hastened demise.

Tommy reached into his back pocket and pulled out his wallet. He flipped through a bunch of cards and papers and such until he found what he had been looking for. He held out a photo and said "Kathleen."

"Kathleen?" I said, beholding what was clearly the high school yearbook picture of a wholly wholesome girl. She radiated a certain kind of hopeful anticipation that was genuinely lovely.

"My high school girlfriend." Tommy said.

"Ah," I said. "She's cute. It's kind of dark in here, but she looks really cute." Kathleen was so open and fresh-faced that her yearbook picture seemed to radiate its own light from her cherubic little cheeks. "So, you're a virgin, then," I added.

He threw his head back and laughed in that really great way he had, but with enough tinge of discomfort that I knew my speculation was right.

"My girlfriend, I should have said," he added.

I looked at him. He put the picture back in his wallet and gave me his big grin.

"Interesting that you amended that," I said. "Are you trying to warn me that you're already 'taken' or trying to remind yourself?"

He laughed. "You're pretty funny," he said.

"You're pretty cagey," I said.

Holy cow, he really *was* a virgin. And no question about Adele, despite her drink order. For a second I thought I might actually blush. A wave of shame washed over me, and I had this feeling like I was so…so…*slutty.* Then I remembered an article my high school friend Nancy had torn out of *Cosmopolitan* magazine. The author was a man, and he was giving advice to young girls and women trying to make their own careful but empowered decisions in navigating their own sexuality post-Sexual Revolution. He had said, "Ladies, rest assured. Being slutty is hardly a bad thing. We *want* you to be slutty!" So my internal pendulum swung the other way, and I felt just about to burst with pride, though I certainly didn't think messing around with two high school boyfriends qualified as slutty. Except, of course, to Catholics. Which Tommy was.

Mostly, I felt bad for Tommy and Adele and grateful to not be a virgin. Bad for them because I figured each of them probably had a highly discouraging, disappointing, awkward, wholly unsatisfying experience ahead of them when their moment came. I could never understand why *anyone* would want to either *be* or be *with* a virgin on their wedding night. If my first sexual experience had been my actual wedding night, I would have crawled into the bathroom and spent the rest of the night crying into the toilet.

I also felt bad for me.

There would be no hair-grabbing, agile-tongued kisses and all of the subsequent etc. between Tommy and me. It wouldn't be right for either one of us. He needed to have a Kathleen, a sweet sweet girl who would cherish every moment of their awkward, mutual exploration. And I needed…well, I really had no idea.

Right about then I felt a looming presence behind my right flank. Tom brushed against my shoulder and plunked down across from me, so close to Adele that she gave him a dirty look before sidling away from him. He didn't notice, which seemed understandable but rude nonetheless. He said nothing, also rude, just put his cigarette between his lips and shimmied his jacket off, then blew the smoke up toward the ceiling. I slid the ashtray over to him and said, "Here. Just in case you want to have your mouth free at some point. Like, for talking or something." He winked at me.

CHAPTER 19

"Esmé, hey, hold up a minute," Ben trotted a couple of steps to catch up. It hadn't registered with me that, on our group stagger back from the bar, Ben hadn't peeled off from the group when Rob did, like he normally would. The two of them used the same dorm entry door. He'd waited until Tom and Tommy had withdrawn, and finally Nina, all of whom had returned to their home ports. Ben and I remained on the sidewalk at the far end of the quad, all by our lonesomes.

One of the important lessons I had already learned was how to hold back my initial impulse to laugh. People said all kinds of things that I thought were hilarious in a wonderfully ironic and arch sort of way. I thought their straight faces were part of the delivery. Ben had been one of most instrumental people in my discovery that these statements were actually *serious* much of the time. When he mentioned that he'd finally figured out a place to set up his ironing board so he could iron his jeans, I literally doubled over in my chair. Ben's facial expression didn't vary from its usual blankness, but his silence and stare made my mistake crystal clear.

"Hey, Ben, what's up? Everything ok?"

"Oh, yeah, sure. Yeah. I was just thinking, I was just wondering, if you'd like to go out sometime?"

"Where were you thinking of going?" I asked.

"Go *out.* You know, on a date."

"On a *date?*" I had no idea how that response came off. I had been caught utterly off guard and am not always so quick on my feet when that is the case, let alone when the situation is painful and absurd in the first place.

"Ben," I said. I went from feeling stunned—and maybe a little put out—to feeling bad and guilty and like I must have done something wrong, and whether I had or I hadn't, in fact, done anything horrible, I now had responsibility for this person. There was this person, this human, standing in front of me and wanting something or needing something, and however ludicrous the need might seem, that was something I needed to be gentle with. That was just the way I wanted to be in the world. I sighed and looked around.

"Well, what do you think?" Ben asked. Ben spoke in an unusually quiet voice—all of the time—and radiated an air of condescension, like he was insisting that you come closer so he could get a better look while he sneered at you.

"I think. I think. I guess I'm not really sure why you're asking me out, Ben. We've hardly ever spoken a word to one another."

"I think you seem to be a fascinating person, Esmé. I'd like to get to get to know you better. I believe that's why people go on dates."

There was a wee small part of me that I did not want to acknowledge, that I wanted to turn my head from, that wanted to say yes to Ben. Ben was one of those people—the not-squirrels. The safety net that ran beneath Ben was so wide and thick and impenetrably tough that the financial life ahead of him was entirely assured. He would take over his grandfather's multi-national conglomerate when the time came. Or he would not take over. And if he did not, if Ben never worked a day in his life, it would make no difference at all in the surety of his future.

My father was most often not home when I went to bed. But on the occasions when he was there, he pulled me onto his lap and read books to me. He held me very close, and he gave me a squeeze each time he turned to a new page. Every detail of the illustrations on each of the pages of *The Little Engine That Could* became etched in my memory, enduring and immutable. Not because I loved the book so much—which I did—but because of the way I felt when my daddy read to me. Completely safe. Protected, cared for, loved, but most of all, safe.

Was this the way that Ben felt?

Was this the way I might feel if I let myself fall into Ben's arms?

"A fascinating person. You think I might be a fascinating person," I said. I wanted to be that person, that person who was unrelentingly kind in the face of human fragility, but I couldn't do it right then. "Here's what I think you really think, Ben. I think you think that I have really long hair. I think that you think that I often don't wear a bra. I think that you think that might just mean that I have sex with lots of different people. I think you think that it's worth a shot to see if that might be true. So you ask me on a date, which I didn't think people still *did* in this day and age, and which conjures up images of poodle skirts and bobby socks and well, now that I think about it, a guy who's dressed pretty much exactly like you're dressed right now, and we slide into a booth across from one another and drink our malts. Anyway, I'm flattered that you asked me, I guess, and even though I've never been on the kind of date I believe you're suggesting, I think I need to decline." I felt awful. Really awful. Ben wasn't a bad person. Well, it's possible that he actually *was* a bad person, but still.

"I hope I don't have a daughter like you, Esmé."

"What?" I was pretty sure I must have heard wrong.

"I said I hope that I don't have a daughter like you," Ben repeated. The weirdest thing was, there didn't seem to be any emotion behind his words. None. He spoke as impassively as if he were making a comment on the nature of watching paint dry.

"Five minutes ago, I'm fascinating, and now you hope you don't have a daughter like me?"

"It seems like it would be so complicated," Ben said. "G'night, Esmé."

CHAPTER 20

"Why are you so nice to everybody?"

I had already passed the person on the staircase. I turned, saw the back of her army jacket facing me and said, "Sorry, are you talking to me?"

"It's just you and me here, cupcake," she said. It was the nightgown girl. Two months into the school year, it was widely believed that she had still not spoken to anyone, except to her professors behind the closed doors of their offices. I felt intrigued, terrified and bemused to have been called "cupcake" by someone I didn't know in the slightest. I tossed my books onto the steps and hesitated for a second or two before I sat down beside her, at a carefully considered distance.

"What do you mean? About me being nice to everyone?"

"Just what I said. It's fucking annoying," she said.

"You're annoyed by my being nice to people?"

"You have a trail of guys following you around like puppies. Most people would kick them," nightgown girl said. "Most of them deserve to be kicked. But you're not a kicker."

"Hi," I said. "I'm Esmé. Nice to meet you. Figured we should introduce ourselves before we get any further into analyzing my behavior patterns."

"I know who you are," she said.

"Great. And I know who you are. Your name's Kendall. But everyone calls you Emily Dickinson."

"'I'm Nobody! Who are you? Are you—Nobody—too?'" Kendall said.

"'Then there's a pair of us!' That poem was stuck in my head the entire first week that I was here," I said. "Weird, huh?"

"Not weird at all. Weirder if it hadn't been stuck," Kendall said. "All things considered."

"You know, you have everyone convinced that you haven't spoken aloud since you got here at the beginning of the year. Ever. Elective muteness. Like Big Chief from *Cuckoo's Nest*."

"Chief Broom," she said. "Big Nurse. Chief Broom. Not Big Chief."

"Oh, my God, I can't believe I got that wrong. That's one of my favorite books of all time," I said.

"Did you do something really bad in a previous life? Something that you're trying to make up for?"

"Not so far as I know," I said, shaking my head.

"See how you're being nice to me right now? Most people take a wide berth. A very wide berth."

"You wear a long white nightgown every single day, Kendall. And combat boots. And the army jacket. Even the first few days of school when it was, like, 150 degrees. Seemed like you were kind of sending a message, a strong 'do not approach' message, especially when you didn't answer anyone who tried to talk to you."

"I'm only talking to you now because I'm going home," Kendall said.

"What do you mean?" I said, and gestured to the dormitory behind us. "You live here. You've lived here for a couple of months."

"No," she said. "I mean home home. Back to my parents."

"Oh," I said. "Oh," I said again. "How come?"

"Cause I'm batshit crazy," Kendall said. "Started seeing funny stuff about a week ago. Stuff that wasn't really there, as it turned out. Thank God for that, too, because it was fucking scary. I'm heavily drugged right now. Wouldn't be talking to you otherwise."

"Oh," I said. I couldn't think of anything to add just then.

"Not seeing weird stuff anymore. So, thank God for that. But I need to go home. Get sorted."

"I'm sorry," I said. "I really am. Sounds awful. And really scary. Shit, Kendall."

"My mother should be here pretty soon," Kendall said.

"I wish you'd decided to talk to me sooner," I said.

"Couldn't do it. But watched; spent a lot of time watching. I like people when I'm watching them from far away. Up close, it's all different. Not enough distance to make sense of anything."

"You might have a good point," I said. "Maybe we all need to spend more time watching."

Kendall stood up. "I got news for you. You can't save everyone. You're adrift. I get that. Just can't save everyone."

With that, Kendall walked past me. Carrying nothing, she walked over to a somber woman whose courage seemed to have faltered. Kendall's mother had stopped just inside the entrance gate to the quad and had not come any farther. When Kendall reached her, the woman put a tentative arm around her daughter. By the time the two of them had walked through the gate, the mother had already pulled her arm away.

I got a pang in my stomach. Crazy or not, I admired Kendall. She knew she was different, and she put it right out there for everyone to see. No one could see the things that made me different. They weren't visible, and I didn't let them be.

I would miss Kendall terribly.

CHAPTER 21

I LOOKED UP FROM THE OPEN BOX THAT SAT ON MY LAP AND said to Tom, "You got me two turtlenecks?" Following a trip home to D.C. for a long weekend to see family and friends, Tom showed up at my dorm room door with a big white box.

Tom didn't say anything, just gestured toward the box and raised both eyebrows. He was a person of such minimal expression, it sometimes made my heart hurt.

"That's really sweet," I said. "I feel like a horrible person; I've never gotten anything for you. Not even a coffee. It's just... my budget is so tight—"

"Hey," he said in a way that made it clear that no more explanation was needed nor would be heard.

"Really sweet," I repeated. "Where did you get them?" I looked at the cover of the box and answered my own question. "Garfinkel's. That's a store in D.C.?"

"Big old downtown store. Beautiful. You'd like it," Tom said.

"Huh," I said.

"Huh, what?" he said. "Was your town too small to have department stores?"

"I don't think anyone could call Crook's a department

store. But…it's more that…it's kind of hard to picture you…wandering around a department store in search of a present. For me."

He didn't feel compelled to respond, apparently.

"Anyway, Tom, you are a man of mystery and surprise. I thank you. Really."

"Took you long enough to say thanks. Didn't your mama raise you good?" I playfully hit him on the head with the box top, and he said, "Apparently, she did not."

Shortly after I clocked Tom on the head, while the box was still on its descent, it hit me: there was only one possible reason a person such as Tom Donahue would wander into, let alone wander around the women's department of Garfinkel's department store in search of a gift for me. That's not the kind of thing you do when you want to get laid. That's the kind of thing you do when you're in love.

Call me naïve, but I had not seen that coming.

Which I suppose meant, really, that I had not wanted—and had ardently hoped—that wouldn't happen. Because I knew that I did not, and would not at any point in the future, feel that same way toward him.

I felt such an enormous sense of sadness, and grief, and guilt and protectiveness, and OK, I had to admit, anger at the utter ruination of any and all fantasies I might have been entertaining about what his snarling, scowling intensity might be like within the context of sexual relations. Between him and me.

He must have seen some degree of what I was feeling on my face because he said, "What?" while raising his eyebrows and gesturing, inevitably, with his eternal cigarette.

"Nothing," I said. "Really."

CHAPTER 22

"WE'RE NOT HERE TO CHANGE THE WORLD, ESMÉ," MONT-gomery Treadwell III said. As if a stage director had cued him, he'd come out of his room just as I was starting up the stairs. I had a batch of flyers under my arm and was on my way to collect Tom or Tommy to distribute them. We were going to hand them out in the dining hall. We wanted to rally our fellow students to protest a debate that the school had scheduled for the coming week. Nobel-prize-winning scientist William Shockley was coming to promote his views on the genetically based intellectual superiority of white folks. He claimed irrefutable proof. He went so far as to actually propose that the United States should offer a *monetary reward* for non-whites to be voluntarily sterilized.

Montgomery had glanced at the flyers, seen the headline spelling out S-h-o-c-k-l-e-y, and figured out what I was up to.

"I was pretty sure that's exactly why we're here," I said. "To change the world. Or at least to try."

He stared at me with no discernible expression. If he'd seemed angry, or contemptuous, or even amused, that would have made more sense to me. I repeated. "At least to try."

"The world doesn't need our saving," he said. "It's already saved. We're here to make sure it stays that way."

WINTER

"I ignored the flashes of lightning all around me.
They either had your number on them or they didn't."

—J.D. Salinger
"For Esmé—with Love and Squalor"

CHAPTER 23

I MOVED TO THE CASTLE IN THE SKY ON JANUARY SECOND, 2020, a Friday. The beginning of a new year, the end of the work week. A hop into the utterly unknown, as is every leap of faith.

The young men from the moving company were a study in brisk yet easygoing efficiency. With a background symphony of paper being wrapped and tape being ripped and boxes being stacked, the four men packed up the material collection of my life history in fewer than three hours. The crew was due for a lunch break before they drove the four miles across town to where they would unload my possessions and hoist them into Gino's castle. I had time to linger in my home of the past twenty-five years, an empty but gleaming jewel of carved woodwork and ceiling beams and crown molding. As there was no furniture remaining, I crammed myself into the dining room's built-in hutch. With its richly aged oak, ornately carved detail that ran the length of the cabinet, and original latches on the glass cabinet doors, mine was one of most gorgeous examples of this architectural feature that I had ever seen. I drank in the feeling of being in a grand old room where various people had lived for more than one hundred years.

I suppose as one gets older, one develops warm feelings for old things that are cherished.

The movers were, once again, a picture of genial competence as they carried the entirety of my belongings out of the moving truck, down the hall, up the freight elevator, down the hallway on the seventeenth floor, and into the aerie. I pointed and directed and accompanied them to the various rooms where my possessions would ultimately be interwoven with Gino's. All of us—the movers and I—kept taking the wrong turn in one of the hallways and finding ourselves back in the living room instead of the bedroom where we had been headed.

I was exhausted by the move, to the marrow of my bones exhausted. Apparently, too worn out to notice my own disorientation in taking all of those wrong turns, and what it may mean. The bottle of champagne Gino and I had chilled for our first night officially living together remained in the refrigerator. I barely managed to toss some food into my mouth before laying my aching, complaining body onto the magnificently embracing mattress and falling into a sleep akin to a coma.

Stoic, noble soul that she was, my beloved dog had kept watch over the comings and goings of the move. When the door closed behind the movers for the final time, I placed her familiar dog bed in an area between the kitchen and the living room where she could gaze out the floor-to-ceiling windows. She laid down, and with a sigh of both relief and pain, claimed the new spot as her own.

"Where am I?"

For the entire period of years that Gino and I had been together, I had never spent the night at his home, which was ridiculous. Gino preferred my neighborhood to his own, so we tended to spend more time at my place from the beginning. But nights were a different matter. The management of Gino's building maintained a strict policy regarding pets: only pets belonging to residents were permitted in the building, and the animals had to be registered and vetted with said management in advance.

This was the first time I had been in this room, in this bed, for the night. It was more of a jolt than a thought. Lying face-to-face with nothingness in a room that was too dark, a dark well beyond that of the room that I had slept in for the past two and a half decades. I glanced in the direction of the clock to orient myself with the anchor of time, but the bright white numbers meant nothing to me. When I grew up, clocks had hands—all of them did; and occasionally, in the night, it took a while for me to translate digital numbers into my own understanding of time.

Ah, but the gentle breathing sounds beside me. The slight rise and fall of the comforter, movement that was not created by me. I sat up and drew my knees toward my chest, amazed at how little I could make out in the blackness of Gino's bedroom. My bedroom now.

A nightlight. We would need a nightlight.

I pictured Gino as a blind man, a blind man who knew his

surroundings so well that lack of sight hindered him not at all. He strode confidently across the bedroom, negotiated the turn into the bathroom, and emptied his bladder with seamless ease before navigating the reverse course back to his bed. Our bed.

On the morning of January third, I made coffee in an unfamiliar pot in an unfamiliar kitchen while Gino slept. I loitered pointlessly around the coffeemaker, uncertain where I would sit and what I would do. Would I transfer my morning routines intact? Make adjustments? Abandon them altogether and create new ones? Hardly the lattermost, as I fully acknowledged the deep entrenchment of my...habits. It was an ongoing disappointment to me that the wisdom that came with my age seemed, so far, confined to my ever-increasing ability to discern each and every one of my bad habits, foibles and general eccentricities while being able to do absolutely nothing to alter them.

I looked out the sea of glass to the sea beyond it. I was well above the treetops, well above my old view where I looked through my first-floor windows to the street, to the earth. That view grounded me, being at the same level as lives lived, just outside my old window, people rooted to the earth in their comings and goings. The people on the stairs so close I could hear their words. I already missed them.

I now looked to a different view to ground me. The harbor beyond my glass castle had frozen solid in the bleak, squat days of the brand-New Year. Beyond the harbor lay the vast lake, stretching to, well, stretching to forever. To the horizon and to the idea of the horizon.

Despite the depth of my attachment to my vintage apartment and the collection of primitive antique furniture which fit it so well, the decision of where Gino and I might live together was not a decision at all. He had considerably more space, nearly twice as much as I had. I had oak-beamed ceilings and original oak doors, but I also had too many stairs and not enough closet space. Too many parts that had warped and shifted over time and needed to be patiently worked around, not unlike Gino and myself. My apartment linked me to a grand architectural past. Gino's linked me—and us—to the distance and possibility of what lay ahead.

Geese trotted along the thin ice where they had swum just days before. I did a double-take then guffawed out loud when I realized that the geese were toddling along the ice in a perfect V-formation, just as if they were soaring through the air. Worried that my laugh might have awakened Gino, I covered my mouth with my hand and stood in the middle of the room having no idea what to do next. In this new house. This new house that was my new house. Morning light flooded the rooms, scattering magnificent patterns of pinkish orange light across the walls and ceilings. A feeling arose in the pit of my stomach and clawed its way up toward my throat. The geese simply could not do it differently. They couldn't even walk across a solid sheet of ice in *any way differently* than they flew. I found myself making great swooshing motions with my arms, as if I could embolden them to break free and run amok. If Gino had not been asleep, it is possible that I would have screamed through the glass. "Step out of formation, dammit! Walk anywhere you want to!!"

I wavered. My prior confidence in the possibilities ahead for me and Gino had been meddled with by the damn geese.

Could I truly expect myself to take in the soul of another human being...again? To love again?

After two more sips of coffee, it occurred to me that I was once again looking to bird behavior for wisdom, and that I really must stop doing that. It also occurred to me that what I had posed was, in fact, a fair question.

The thin sheets of ice had formed fissures, cracks that divided the harbor into tectonic plates of distinct islands with amorphous coastlines. I thought of the Leonard Cohen song: there is a crack in everything; that's how the light gets in.

I saw Leonard Cohen perform, late in his life. His smooth rapport with his audience and with his bandmates. Understated, pithy, casually eloquent. I later learned that Cohen carefully scripted every single word that he said during his stage performances, and he repeated that same script at every show for that entire tour. Every word of that seemingly casual banter had been laid out, edited, rehearsed, repeated. I felt cheated at first, when I learned this. Betrayed by the knowledge that he said the exact same things to *us,* this audience that he seemed so genuinely enchanted by. His vintage sports coat and natty fedora beautifully mirroring the magnificently restored theatre where he was performing; he had said these identical things to countless others. And then it hit me. He wasn't a jerk; he was a writer. A zealous believer in the power of words. Cohen took a vow of silence at one point in his life to see what could be learned from a *lack* of words. His entire life was centered on words—their presence or their absence—how he might arrange them to reflect our dreams and our agonies.

The ground vs. the sky. The near at hand vs. the boundless. I thought about how my view—the world in front of my eyes each time I glanced up—would affect the things that went on inside of me. How might I be changed, being high up, far away, by having a vastness before my eyes?

Here is the thing.

My father was gone when I was so young.

And I had kept a secret for such a long time.

I would always be lonely.

CHAPTER 24

IT'S TOO LATE. I'M HOLDING PINKBUNNY BY HIS LITTLE PAW.
*There's no stuffing left in the top of his arm, just cloth, but his
paw is full as ever. Mom says he's too used up, and I'm too big
now anyway, to keep him and sleep with him still. Daddy says,
"Nonsense, Anne, as long as pinkbunny is special to Esmé, pinkbunny sticks around." He winks at me, and he winks at Mom,
too. But I keep pinkbunny in my room now if I think someone besides Daddy and Mom might be around, because I don't
want anybody to say anything that might make Mom change
her mind and decide that he's too used up after all. It's too late
now, though. They've already seen him.*

*It's so early in the morning, why is Dr. McClelland here? Why
is he sitting on the couch with Mom? They look over at me, both
of them, at exactly the same time. They look surprised, no, more
like caught, like I have caught them at something, like I have
caught them being naughty. Mom's eyes are small and pink, and
her nose is bright, bright red, like when she has a really bad
cold in her head. "Esmé," she says, and I have never heard her
voice like this, it is different, like she doesn't have enough air. She
folds her hands in her lap, all of her fingers laced together, like
she is going to say a prayer.*

"Come here, Esmé," Dr. McClelland says. He holds his arms out to me, and I know that I'm supposed to do what he says, I'm supposed to go over to him; but everything is so strange and doesn't make sense. I'm scared and I want my daddy, I just want my daddy like I always do when I feel scared. I walk really slowly over to him, and when I get close enough, he lifts me onto his lap. I am more scared than ever when he does this. He clears his throat and breathes really loud, and I can smell him. I can smell his breath that's coming through his nose and also some kind of clean soap or perfume that's coming from his face. And I think he just shaved because his cheeks have that look like Daddy's do, all shiny and smooth with no little tiny hairs at all, just faint little dots where hairs will come out later.

"I have some very sad news, sweetheart," he says. He is my doctor and has never ever called me "sweetheart" or anything like that before, so I know that the news must be awful, bad, terrible news. "Your daddy had a heart attack last night; and I know that you don't know what that is—"

"Yes, I do," I said. "I do know what that is."

"Well, it's very unusual for a person as young as your father to have a heart attack, but it does happen. And your father had a heart attack last night, and the heart attack killed him. He died, and he's gone to heaven with the angels."

Mom pushes her lips together in a funny way and whimpers kind of like a puppy. I look at her face, but she doesn't look at me. She looks straight down into her lap, right at her hands. They look like they've been glued together into the prayer position, like she couldn't move her fingers if she tried.

Dr. McClelland looks over at her, too, then back at me. He smiles a little smile then wipes it off his face like maybe that wasn't the right thing to do. He looks at Mom again.

A secret. That's what it was. They looked like two people who had a secret—when I first came into the room.

But I had a secret, too. My secret envelope.

I needed to learn how to read right away so I could figure out what Daddy had said to me.

CHAPTER 25

It is amazing the lies we can tell ourselves—how fully we can convince ourselves, fool ourselves into believing that various things about us are true. With a spirit of creativity and a zest for denial, I managed to bend and twist my great dislike of eating alone into a belief that I never actually did it.

During the years and years that I had lived essentially alone—not counting the assortment of men who skittered in and out of my life at various points—I lost all love for cooking. This happenstance came about gradually, mostly stemming from my dislike of eating by myself. For someone who relished my solitude and protected it with the ferocity of a snow leopard in the high Himalayas, everything changed the second food became involved. By the time I met Gino, I had gradually convinced myself that I wasn't actually eating meals alone. I wasn't in my dining room, wasn't sitting at a table, and hadn't done any cooking. I was simply relaxing on my couch while catching up on some reading. Playing the odd computer game while leafing through a catalog. Making notes of particularly interesting snippets uttered by the people on the stairs. The large plates of food in front of me were merely generous snacks. After all, I was balancing them on my lap. Hence: snacks. It felt perfectly acceptable to grab a quick snack alone while doing at least one other activity.

Buried deep, hibernating inside of my memory, remained a visceral, sensual longing to once again thrust my own hands into *food* that I was preparing, food that I would later eat with people that I loved. Within me existed a slumbering symphony: muscle memory of a kitchen abuzz. Knives chopping, oil sizzling, oven doors opening and closing, the whoosh of gas burners igniting. A humming opus of color and sound and warmth that melded together into…*aroma*. Working a pie crust, for instance, from its beginnings as a bowlful of powder and greasy lumps, kneading the mixture between each of my fingers until it resembled coarse sand. How I longed to keep working the nascent crust, to keep fingering the sandy miracle, but I knew that I needed to stop just as soon as the mixture started to hold together into a dough. If I didn't stop kneading, the crust would be over-handled, tough. I would squish the dough one last time between each of my fingers, then hold up my hands and admire the gloppy dough that made the hard-worked fingers into enormous, comical, bright white appendages. There is nothing, not one thing, that can match the aroma of a home-baked pie. The first whispers floating through the air, just hints, causing the hairs inside one's nose to stand at full attention, tickling the brain, teasing, stronger then stronger still, until one's head is teeming with the sensuality of *aroma* that the melding ingredients radiate.

Despite my ongoing apprehension about moving in together after living alone for multiple decades, I was so looking forward to cooking again, and to eating dinner with Gino every night. We could once again call it *dinner*. We would eat... *dinner*. We would sit at a gargantuan table fabricated from concrete that Gino had custom-made for the space.

Of all the treasured possessions I had given up when Gino and I painstakingly combed through and winnowed down our combined furniture, the decision to give away my Shaker dining table stung the most. Though it was quite damaged, it was a precious part of my past. I couldn't bear the thought of selling it, of money being exchanged for so precious a part of my history. Instead, I ran a classified ad with a photo of the table and asked interested parties to write a note or story that would inspire me to choose them as the new owner. The winning candidate submitted a brief but stunning story of the table's nearly 100-year history, told from the point of view of the table itself—how somber and tedious it had been to be surrounded by Shakers—people who isolated themselves, believing that life should be focused on work and should be free of any desire—only to get the last laugh when Shaker style was adopted by cash-loaded young dot-commers who would gladly stab one another's eyes out to nab a particularly fine piece.

Even considering my strong predilection for antiquities, I liked Gino's table quite a lot and agreed that it suited the overall space perfectly.

Visions of Gino and me preparing meals together danced in my head. He would chop. I would stir. We would sip red wine and gesture casually with our glasses. I would admire the way his rear end looked in his jeans, noting how much it… stirred the senses to cook together. I was quite excited, but I knew that Gino had lost the concept of cooking and eating at home as well. In the five years since his wife died, Gino left his office each evening and went straight to one of his extensive list of favorite restaurants. He took his time with his meal, read the *New York Times* from cover to cover, and honed his people-watching and eavesdropping skills to a level any writer would admire and envy.

I knew that we needed to proceed slowly. I knew that I needed to turn down the intensity level of my own zeal a couple of notches; Gino was a gentle soul who had grown used to a quiet and orderly life. We would start small—a simple trip to the closest grocery store. I figured we could lay in a few basic supplies, begin to stock the pantry with items we'd use over time. We made it all the way through the produce section and to the canned tomato aisle without incident, though Gino was unusually quiet. The perfectly stacked rows upon rows of whole, crushed, chopped, pureed, fire roasted, sun dried, garlic added, herbs added, fire roasted garlic added. My head was awash with a universe of tomato-based sauces, and I felt woozy from visions of cooking euphoria. Gino, meanwhile, was standing exceptionally close to one particular can of fire roasted tomatoes and seemed to be breathing heavily. "Gino," I said, "For heaven's sake, is everything OK?"

He said, "Mmm," as if to indicate a *yes,* and he backed slowly away from the can and pushed the cart ahead.

"I thought you looked a little pale earlier. You feeling all right?"

He raised one arm in a thumbs up, his back turned. He continued to push the cart. I shrugged, to the tomatoes I suppose, and shuffled along to catch up with him.

Once home, we unloaded the multitude of grocery bags and lined the contents up on the kitchen counters. Gino walked over to the pantry and opened the double doors while I architecturally arranged the frozen goods. But when I closed the door to the freezer and started talking to Gino, last seen at the pantry, he wasn't there. I called his name. No answer.

We were brand-new in our living together and very much in the initial stages of learning one another's daily habits. I figured he must have made a dash for the bathroom. But the bathroom door was wide open, and we did not have an open-door policy regarding certain bathroom activities at that point in our relationship. I continued to call Gino's name as I wandered around the apartment, finally coming to a dead stop at the bedroom door.

Gino was sitting at the edge of the bed, his head between his knees, breathing into a brown paper bag.

"Oh, my God, what's going on?" I was panicked. Terrifying visions that my long-sought possibility for lasting love might perish the very first week of our living together flashed through my petrified brain.

His head still inside the bag, Gino nodded and held up his index finger, a gesture to indicate that he needed more time.

"Tell me what to do," I said. "What can I do?"

He pulled his head out of the bag and threw himself onto the bed. "All those *ingredients*," he said.

"Ingredients?" I was, quite frankly, baffled.

"We have to *use* them now! So many…*ingredients*."

Gino continued to breathe in great, uneven gasps, his hand held across his heart.

"Wait. What?" I asked.

"It was one thing when you were piling them into the cart. But now they're in our *house*. All of those…*things!*" he said.

Gino cleared his throat and looked at me. I could not help it; I burst out laughing. "Sweetheart," I said, "are you saying that you're scared of the *groceries?*" I sat down beside him on the bed.

"There are so many of them. When I open the refrigerator now, there are *things* in there. It feels like so much pressure. *Pressure!* You know. To use them!"

"You feel pressured by the groceries," I said, in a tone that I recognized as the comforting but perturbed tone that one would use with an irrational child.

"Yes!" Gino said. And again, "Yes!"

I had no idea what to say. He fiddled with the bag. I patted his leg

"Does this happen very often, by the way? This paper bag thing? Just curious."

"No. Not very." Gino was sheepish by this time, and back to his usual self.

Whereas it would have been difficult for me to abide a man who didn't intend to do a reasonable share of the cooking, I could certainly respect a good old-fashioned nutty idiosyncrasy: a dread of ingredients. As a lifelong devotee of unusual quirks and eccentricities, I found this wonderfully endearing, and I loved him all the more.

CHAPTER 26

I LAID SPREAD-EAGLE ON A KING-SIZED BED THAT SEEMED even larger than they usually do. "I am never moving. Not ever. This is my spot," I said to Gino. Gino sat on a sliver of the bed's edge and stroked my ankle. "Don't touch me yet. Give me a few more minutes to cool down," I implored. Gino snatched his hand back like a snake had bitten him, and I laughed. "I'm sorry," I said. "I know how much this means to you. I'm sorry I'm being such a baby about the heat."

Gino was a huge fan of the warm-weather-getaway winter vacation. Even though I was still very much getting my bearings in our new comingled home, Gino ardently wanted to swoop me off to someplace tropical. "I'll do all the work," he had said. "All of the planning. I'll run everything by you, or I can totally surprise you. Your choice."

"Boxes," I said in response. "There are still boxes in the spare room. Boxes we haven't touched yet…." If Gino could be charmingly neurotic about ingredients, I could be irrational about the urgency of unpacking boxes that had been untouched since my previous move, some twenty-five years earlier.

"You did the lion's share of the work with the move. You deserve it, and I think you need it. We both need it. You need to relax, and I need to be warm. Even better: Hot. Baking, blazing hot."

Certainly, this presented a dilemma. It's many a woman's dream to have her male partner plan *anything* whatsoever, let alone *everything*. That's the stuff of romance novels and fantasies women divulge to one another after the second round of drinks. On the other hand, part of the reason that writers write is because they can, thereby, control everything. Every. Single. Detail.

I also knew that, despite a degree of self-interest, it was a lovely offer on Gino's part, a genuine desire to care for me in a way that had been so long absent.

In the end, we compromised. Gino did the background research based on my peculiar predilections: smaller, out-of-the-way places that respected both the environment and the native people in their construction and ongoing management. He flashed photos in front of me that I regarded with my eyes half closed, rendering the pictures blurry. I figured I had seen just enough to be able to give my heartfelt approval, but little enough to enable me to be entirely surprised by the reality when the time came.

Sadly, the reality commenced the second I stepped from the actual airplane and into the gangway. Enough searing, steamy heat had insinuated itself through the minimal spaces between the plane and the portable gangway that I felt like I'd been slapped by an ocean wave whose power was too much for me to survive. Gino's face had relaxed—noticeably—and the corners of his mouth tended upward in a way that I had not seen before. He was already in heaven.

I took one look at the long lines to get through customs and what seemed to be an inadequately scant number of officials, and I felt like shouting, "Halleluiah!" The bafflingly gigantic room was approximately the temperature of the average refrigerator. People were tearing open their carryon bags and donning fleeces and sweatshirts and jackets in a symphony of sound and movement.

I wanted to stay in the airport. Forever. I knew it was an absurd notion, but nonetheless.

I drew out my love affair with the frosty airport for as long as I could with two trips to the rest room, a suggestion that we exchange our American cash so we would not have to worry about it later, and a further suggestion that we really should browse a few shops to stock up on…well, I couldn't really think of anything in particular. But I proposed that our lodgings were sufficiently remote that we might want to see if we spotted anything that seemed like it could be useful.

The posh eco lodge had arranged transportation from the airport for us.

I had focused on the concept of posh and not so much on the concept of eco, though it had been my choice.

Likewise, I had focused on the concept of posh and not on the concept of its commitment to the local community, though it had also been my choice.

Even when I saw the man holding up the sign with our name on it, my hopes remained intact.

Then he led us to the car, and I immediately put it together: commitment to the local community translated into hiring an eager, hard-working, congenial youngster who happened to have access to a "car." And I remembered that nearly everyone in this part of the world got their cars used—*very* used—when they already had several hundred thousand miles on them. We were headed back to the era of hand-cranked windows, dubious seat beats, and no air conditioning.

It was a two-hour journey.

When we pulled out of the airport parking lot, Gino turned into a Labrador retriever who had finally been allowed to put his head out the window. I tried, I yearned to let the expanse of Gino's unfettered delight fill me. I wanted to breathe in his joy the way he breathed in the tropical air. Once the sweat began running in large streams between my breasts and soaking the belly of my shirt, I officially gave up trying.

The road was paved for the first hour of our trek. Less than five minutes after the asphalt ended with an abrupt two-inch thud down to the dusty, gravelly "road," I had already developed a nostalgia for the original highway's gentler handling of my sopping self.

Gino squeezed my hand periodically in a lovely gesture of sympathy at my plight. We knocked from side to side and up and down in the dust-choked back seat in silence—stunned silence, in my case, and blissful silence in Gino's. The road traversed dense, wooded jungle, the stifling monotony broken only by our driver's periodic explosion of the word, "Monkeys!!" accompanied by elaborate gesturing.

We gave the exuberant youngster an extremely generous tip when he deposited us in what looked like the absolute middle of uninterrupted jungle save for a tasteful little sign that said "Reception" with an arrow that seemingly pointed… nowhere. Gino and I turned our heads to look at the sign, then back toward the youngster at exactly the same time, as if we had rehearsed this synchronized precision movement. The youngster nodded and pointed animatedly, and said, "You go! I bring luggage!"

Gino and I crept in the direction of the sign. Sure enough, when we were practically standing on top of the sign itself, there lay a flagstone, and below it, another. Each flagstone stair was larger than the one before it. As the stones became more massive, the staircase wound its way around a corner. On the bottommost step, we found ourselves on an enormous veranda. Our jaws dropped, our movements, once again, in perfect unison. Even in my sodden, sorry state, my mouth did, indeed, fall open in awe. The veranda had been constructed atop a high bluff that commanded a panoramic view of the ocean below, the crescent-shaped beach of an enormous cove, the forest that sprang up behind the beach, and the mountains that rose beyond the forest. Waves broke thunderously below, and mountains soared above—undeveloped, pristine land as far as the eye could see.

"Welcome!" A woman rose from behind a desk that had clearly been fabricated by hand from local wood. "You must be hot and tired from your travels. Please! Have a seat and allow me to bring you a cool drink, if I may."

She ducked into a side room and disappeared momentarily when she opened a refrigerator door. When the door closed, she re-emerged with two coconut shells on a tray, each of which contained a straw, a skewer of fresh fruit, and an orchid. Between the heat and the awe, both Gino and I were essentially non-verbal. We mumbled our thanks and took deep swigs from our straws. Whatever we drank from those coconuts was blessedly, restoratively freezing cold. But when the heavenly sensation of the coolness stepped aside, we experienced a taste that was divinity itself. Just as Gino and I were attempting to relocate our verbal ability to share our rapture, she was back, standing beside us with another tray.

"I have taken the liberty of bringing you cold towels. We keep them in the freezer, but they thaw quickly. I think you will find them very refreshing. We use ylang ylang to give them just a slight fragrance."

I felt torn. Reaching for the towel required me to put down my beloved coconut shell drink, and I was loath to do that. The very thought of it caused me to unconsciously snatch the coconut toward my chest, but the delicious scent of the ylang ylang had reached me. I put the drink down and buried my entire face in the cold towel. It was nothing short of a miracle. I ran the cloth up and down both arms then ran it around the full circle of my neck. Gino did the same. There the two of us sat, drinks in our hands, cool towels encircling our necks, under the massive palapa roof that shaded us while we gazed at an unspoiled slice of our planet's splendor.

"Please feel free to stay here as long as you'd like." She was back again. "Enjoy the view. You may want to rest a while before we show you to your accommodations. You have a beautiful room with the same view as we have here. But to get there, you go down the stairs to the beach and then back up a different set of stairs to reach your room."

"Stairs?" I said.

"Yes, there are stairs down to the beach—you can stop and see the beach if you like—then some stairs to your room," she said.

"Some?" I said.

"A few stairs," she said.

"A few?" I said.

"You will see. It's very beautiful. You can rest as much as you like."

I could feel my shoulders slump. I could feel my entire spirit slump. "Let's just do it," I said to Gino. He nodded his assent, and I turned to the lovely, gracious woman who was the architect of my doom and said, "We'll go now."

CHAPTER 27

I LAY THERE ON THE BED IN THE ROOM THAT WE HAD FINALLY finally reached after *a few stairs,* feeling mighty sorry for poor Gino needing to abide my tetchiness, but so much sorrier for my poor self. I remained motionless and stared straight up, fearing that even the slightest movement would increase the already torrential amount of moisture exuding from every bit of me. I had begun to fear that I might grow mold.

"Hey, what's that *thing* above me? Up there?" I made a very slight upward movement of my chin as I spoke.

"Up where?" Gino said. "On the ceiling?"

"No, no. *Right* above my head. That thing that looks like the bed is wearing a hoodie," I said.

Gino's eyes locked onto the bed hoodie—a tautly stretched sheet of white fabric encased in a plastic frame—that reached up from the headboard and loomed about six feet above the mattress. "Huh," Gino said. "Never seen anything quite like that. You?"

"Well, no, that's why I asked." A sad thought flitted into my head and stuck its tongue out at me. I wondered if I would exert the same amount of effort that I was exerting right then—to be civil to Gino—if this scene were to occur many years into our relationship. I hoped so. I hoped I could think of myself as that decent of a human being.

Gino had begun to scrounge around the bedside tables where a bounty of informative placards had been arranged for our perusal. He picked one of them up and said, "Ha!" And after a brief pause, "HaHA!" Holding the placard in his hand for comparison, he retrieved one of several remote controls that also graced the bedside table, hit a couple of buttons with great emphasis, and said, "Voilà, my darling. Now we are truly in heaven."

Once Gino discovered that the strange bed hoodie was actually an air conditioning system that blew a gentle but solidly cool and dry breeze directly onto our prone bodies, everything changed.

The rest of our time melted into a dreamy blur. Days under a beach palapa with the surf torrid and pounding. Days without a whisper of breeze, the waves barely interrupting the aqua expanse. Walks. Hikes. Books. Fresh, delicious food in abundance. Languid, creaky lovemaking. And always the view. On the beach, with the flat infinity of water on one side and the world rising in steep lushness, encircling the other side. Or the opposite view, from the veranda, from our room. A mountain-top view of the earth, water, and the sky that we had become a part of.

A whisper at dinner on our last night there.

Had we heard?…

Gino and I looked at one another but kept walking.

We passed them, every so often, people whose faces were covered from the bridge of their noses to below their chins. Only their eyes visible, but no one made eye contact.

"What do you think we should do?" Gino asked me.

"I don't know," I said. "What do you think?"

Gino said nothing. We kept going. After a while, Gino said, "Maybe we should try to find some."

"Maybe it's a good idea," I said.

We dragged our suitcases to vendor after vendor, all of which had posted signs: "NO Masks. SOLD OUT."

A couple noticed us regarding the sign, dejection undoubtedly radiating from us, and said, "Ice cream shop. Right over that way. We were just there."

Gino and I had not seen so many people in more than a week. Even such a small airport seemed jammed with bodies. A tumbled mass of humanity. A thought slithered inside of us: the whisper we had heard at dinner. Something insidious and dangerous might be creeping among us.

Information poured in. News updates tripped and stumbled over one another in a ceaseless cascade, and the whole world watched.

"What do you think we should do?" I asked Gino.

"I don't know," he said. "What do you think?"

Six days after our tropical vacation ended with Gino and me wearing blue surgical masks on the flight home, our city and our state went into lockdown. We were told to stay home.

Only one person in our home state of Illinois had gotten sick so far. Nonetheless, Gino and I had decided to stay home a week before our mayor and our governor made their grim announcement. We were heading into lockdown.

By the last day of the month of March, twenty-three people had died.

1 9 7 4

" 'Dear God, life is hell.' "

—J.D. Salinger
"For Esmé—with Love and Squalor"

CHAPTER 28

IT WAS HARD, REALLY HARD, TO GO BACK TO THAT SCHOOL AF-
ter holiday break. Mom and I had agreed that the plane ticket
home, plus getting a really big, beautiful Christmas tree to
decorate, would be our only presents to each other. Mom and
I both knew that either one of us was likely to break our word
and buy one or two gifts anyway, so we had to double pinky
extra promise swear that we wouldn't.

It amazed and saddened me somehow to see how the long
drive that Mom and I had made together in the fall could be
reduced to a lightning-fast plane ride. I hadn't had enough
time to consider getting bored or uncomfortable—even
though I was wedged between two people and therefore destined to spend the entire flight pretending to be asleep. In no
time at all, I was wandering around the massive airport in a
swarm of post-holiday scurrying, trying to find the van service that would take an additional two to three hours to reach
the college—longer than the flight had been. Once the driver
had taken my small duffle and carelessly tossed it into the
cargo area, I settled myself in the far corner of the far back
seat. I turned my whole body toward the window, one of the

many tools in my repertoire of discouraging strangers from talking to me.

It was at least an hour into my drowsy, unfocused stare at the passing cottage communities. Every so often, I would focus my gaze and watch the patterns my breath made as I exhaled on the van window. The pleasant stupor had done a pretty fair job of softening the creeping despair I had felt in the airport. I had stopped bothering to turn my head when the van made its stops, no longer curious about the comings and goings of others.

"Esmé." The voice hit me like the crazy sonic booms I remembered from my childhood—right in the chest. You never saw the plane. There would just be this voluble, deep thunder, like the world had split apart, then the feeling of something hitting you—right in the chest. I knew whose voice it was without looking.

"Hey. Ben." The only remaining seat in the van, thank God, was way up in front, next to the driver. I guessed there wasn't any more room in the cargo area either, because Ben had quite a time trying to wedge his two large bags into the front and then wedge himself in. I shouted up to him, "I don't think it's a whole lot farther, is it?"

"I'm ok," he said, sneer dripping from his strangely hushed voice. Sneer always dripped from Ben's strangely hushed voice.

"Did you have a good break? Good holidays?" I asked him.

He didn't have time to answer before the driver restarted the van engine and further talking became doomed. Ben gave me a little shrug and a little wave and turned his back to me.

Whatever relief I felt at the prospect of not having to chit-chat with Ben for an hour or more was far overshadowed by the realization that I was, in fact, returning to a cloistered world with a large number of Bens.

CHAPTER 29

"SERIOUSLY, YOU'RE ABOUT THE TENTH PERSON I'VE RUN INTO in the four blocks from the art building," I said to Rob.

"Well, hello to you, too, Sunshine," Rob said. He shuffled his feet, just once, like he always did, then combed his fingers through his amazingly thick hair, like he always did. It was that gesture—the fingers through the hair—that got me. Every time since the night I had met him along with the Tommy Twins. It brought out something weird and maternal that I didn't even know was there. I just wanted to…I don't know, hug him or adopt him or follow him around and make sure that nobody hurt him, ever. It was sort of like I felt with the engineers—that there was something so exquisite and lovely and fragile that I couldn't bear the thought of that precious-ness being buffeted around by the ever-accumulating dam-ages of life.

"Seriously, I think I belong at a bigger school. I think I yearn to be anonymous," I said.

"I don't think the coat is doing you any favors," he said. "Not if you want to be anonymous."

"Oh, my God. Not with the coat again! Haven't you gotten enough mileage out of this coat?"

"I think the horse got enough mileage out of the blanket before they even made it into a coat," he said. "Really, I'm counting on an early spring."

"It's a good thing I'm not sensitive or fragile or anything 'cause this would be deeply wounding to me," I said.

"Are you taking an art class, by the way? I didn't know you were taking an art class."

"No, no art class. The art school cafeteria has these amazing bran muffins." He stared blankly at me. "They warm them up for you." I fought back a tear. Crazy that I was so powerfully moved by the idea of someone warming a muffin for me.

"Bran muffins," he said, deadpan, as if to indicate this was one of the more puzzling things he had heard.

"Don't judge the muffin. You can judge the coat, but you cannot judge the muffin," I said. There was another "me" that stood outside of myself. I watched myself as I stood on that exact spot near the far corner of the freshman quad, under the eternally gray sky, wrapped in the coat that Rob loathed. I found it amazing that I could appear so normal. The whirl inside of me did not show.

"Promise me that you'll give me the coat as soon as the weather warms. I'm going to personally donate it to Salvation Army. No way I can face the possibility of looking at that coat again next winter."

Next winter. It was when he said "next winter" that I knew. Right then, I knew.

There would be no "next winter" for me. I would not be coming back to this school.

I thought of the wrenching, poignant play *A Memory of Two Mondays*. Arthur Miller tells the story of a young man who goes to work in an auto parts factory to save money for college. The young man is passing through, working alongside an entire group of people who were there long before he arrived and who will remain long after he is gone. He and another co-worker are charged with the task of cleaning the filthy factory windows. The passage of time is told by the light on the stage set, which gets incrementally brighter as more of the windows get cleaned. The light shines into the dismal scene. The young man's mood, like mine, gets brighter and brighter as the light changes and he knows that the end of his time at the factory is near. He also knows that those he leaves behind—the bitter, the resigned, the angry, the uncertain, and even the content—have a bond, a sense of unity, that has never included him.

Neither a Ben, nor a Montgomery, Rob was one of the good ones. A good one that I would not get to know much better than I had and might never see again after the end of the year.

I considered telling him my recent decision, but I didn't. I was not sure why.

"See you at dinner?" Rob asked.

"See you at dinner," I said.

CHAPTER 30

I TOOK A DEEP BREATH BEFORE ENTERING THE OFFICE OF DR. David Ackerman, wunderkind professor who had shepherded the ten of us special English program kids through more than half of our year-long seminar.

I liked my fellow students. But as the year had unfolded, I had come to think of them in much the same way as I thought of some kids back in Clarion—the ones that I babysat to earn my spending money. They were all smart and had interesting things to say. I couldn't wait to hear what came out of their mouths much of the time. I was mesmerized by their gestures and tics and idiosyncrasies. Anna, for instance, flushed impressively after just a few sips of sherry each week. With a few sips more, she snorted each time she laughed and no longer covered her mouth with her hand. Precious little treasures of humanity. They all had them, and I cherished them.

They just seemed so *young*. Well, not young exactly. More like…untroubled. As if nothing bad had ever happened to them. As if they'd managed to make it to the age of eighteen without trauma or tragedy. They were trauma virgins. Untouched.

We'd spent three or four hours each week sipping sherry and writing papers and gabbing our way through literary icons going all the way back to *Beowulf* (sheesh), *Oedipus Rex* (a ripping yarn), creeping into later centuries with works such as *Paradise Lost* (loved it!), and (finally) skyrocketing into the 20th Century with *Death in Venice* and *The Metamorphosis* (both brilliant!). Punchline: we all knew that Dr. David was a renowned James Joyce scholar. We all knew that the entire second semester would be devoted to the great passion of Ackerman's life—*Ulysses.* Pretty sure that all of us had read *Portrait of the Artist as a Young Man* (loved it!). I'd also read *The Dubliners* and liked it fine.

I was completely unprepared for my utter hatred of *Ulysses.* Utter. Hatred. Not just a moderate dislike or middling disinclination. I despised it so much that Oedipal fantasies of stabbing my eyes out and Kafkian visions of transforming into a cockroach became comforting. Anything that kept me from having to read, analyze, dissect, interpret this dreaded book for another second, let alone the rest of the entire semester. Not to mention having to write a major paper on it.

How do you tell a guy who has devoted his academic career to one particular work that you hate, loathe, despise, detest and abhor that same particular work?

After considerable deliberation, I included a handwritten note with one of the papers I turned in saying that, due respect, *Ulysses* was not destined to be counted among my favorite books and, due respect, was there any possibility that I could do my major project on a different book? He, in turn, handed back my paper the following week with a note of his own. He suggested that I read the final chapter and see if I continued to feel the same way. In either event, I should schedule a meeting with him.

Hence, there I was, standing stock still outside of Ackerman's office, taking a deep breath and organizing my thoughts. And fretting that the palms of my hands were so sweaty that actual drops of liquid might begin to form and drip down noticeably. I took one final deep breath and mentally scanned my views on the famous final chapter, Molly Bloom's soliloquy and well yes who doesn't like a clever stream of consciousness yes and I can get behind an e e cummings type complete lack of punctuation and yes innovations abound in the telling and yes yes it grabbed me far more than anything else in the book but yes that is a decidedly low bar and yes I tried I really really yes yes tried to like this book but I must ask that I be freed from this seminal work of literature yes I ask you again yes.

It's hard to say exactly what happened once Dr. David Ackerman ushered me into his appropriately professorial, book-packed gem of an office and sat down behind the most beautiful antique desk I had ever seen. I was working so hard to articulate my thoughts on *Ulysses* without resorting to words such as swamp and drivel and effete, words that continually flashed through my brain like neon signs.

I did not want to be unkind. I wanted to say my piece without shitting on my professor's passion. I did not want to say that, no, sorry, a repressed male Irish Catholic author trying to paint the excited female mind does not balance out the rest of the book for me. No.

I sank deep into what I recognized as defensive babble, so

I'm not certain at what point Dr. David Ackerman got up from behind the exquisite desk. I have no idea what I might have been saying when he went to the Gothic leaded-glass window and closed the shades. Nor when he took off his sports coat, removed his tie, and rolled up the sleeves of his striped dress shirt. He did that each week in class, after all, unless the room was unusually cold. It registered—only slightly—when he walked behind me and flicked the switch to turn off the overhead light.

It was when he walked back behind his desk, when he oozed himself into his chair, that I snapped into focus. I stopped talking. In a nearly dark room, I watched in stunned silence as Dr. David Ackerman leaned way, way back in his chair, placed his interlaced hands behind his head, and looked at me with what in a bad and trite novel would be called "bedroom eyes." And then. And then, he started flexing his bicep muscles. Dark room. Bedroom eyes. Flexing biceps.

Was he *serious?* Was my English professor actually coming on to me!? I felt sick and horrified and shocked and disgusted and…and…disgusted.

I had never understood the whole younger woman/older man phenomenon; and even though Dr. David Ackerman was probably fewer than twenty years older than I was, that made him not so different in age than my Clarion friends' *dads.* My stomach clenched, and I thought I may well vomit, possibly right down the front of his carefully unbuttoned shirt. I hadn't grown up around very many older men, so guys who were even a few years older than I was had seemed *ancient* to me.

Even guys who'd recently finished college and come home to Clarion—back when I was in high school—seemed wizened and withered and crinkly somehow. I couldn't imagine them *touching me*. That just seemed gross.

But this was worse. So much worse than just gross.

This was wrong.

Was I supposed to feel flattered?

Was I supposed to feel excited, turned on, wild with desire over the prospect of having a fling with the renowned wunderkind Joyce scholar sherry drinker?

I felt none of those things.

I felt sick.

I felt sad.

I looked at Dr. David Ackerman and saw a man who was so full of himself that he spent a great deal of his time waiting for the world to catch up with his own view of his luminous place in the universe. I saw a man who couldn't even imagine that the undergrad-of-the-moment would be anything less than weak-kneed at the prospect of being the focus of his attention. I saw a man who, once I ignored or rejected his advances—which I wholly intended to do—would shrug it off without a second thought as being entirely my loss. He would set his sights elsewhere. He would move on. He would prey on another student after me. And another and another.

But I...I was destined to sit in his class for several more months, sipping sherry, looking around at my fellow students and feeling the ever-deepening chasm between them and me. An open, gaping mouth of a chasm, with sharp teeth. Me teetering on the edge.

CHAPTER 31

It was after 4:00 pm when I dragged my sorry self—and I mean sorry in so many different ways—out of bed and into a standing position. I was immediately unsure why I had bothered. Then I remembered. It was Sunday, and there was no food available anywhere on campus after the swanky Sunday brunch closed down. None. Anywhere. The surrounding carcass of a once-proud colonial city had surprisingly few options that were open on Sundays either, and the paltry selection of one diner, one pizza joint and a forlorn little donut shop closed early as well. If I wanted to get anything in my stomach before the next morning, I needed to get out there and forage.

I tossed on my old pink bathrobe and knotted the tired belt around my poor, alcohol-abused middle. I pulled the edges of the collar up around my face to burrow, like I always did. I hadn't washed the robe for a while, and the smell of *me* that suffused the fraying terry cloth, faint as it was from my brief daily wear, was enough to cause a small retch, the harbinger of the awful possibility that I might be sick again. Again again.

The only thing that might possibly help, and the only thing I could possibly consider putting in my mouth, was the Hangover Donut at the hole in the wall donut shop about half a mile away. And a giant coffee. The biggest cup they had in the whole place. I was in such rough shape that I seriously considered throwing my winter coat right on top of my bathrobe. The coat fell to just below my knees; an extra foot or more of pink bathrobe would hang down below the coat, which did not seem like much of a big deal right then. Plus, there was so little daylight at this point in the godforsaken winter that it was almost dark already. Plus, I was mad. At everyone and everything. If my fellow students saw me and decided I was a dangerous lunatic who had gone completely around the bend, that suited me just fine. If the townsfolk saw me and thought I was yet another deranged, derelict part of the generalized urban blight, that struck me as just fine, too. As long as no one decided to hit me with their fucking baseball bat. Or worse. No reason to think about worse, though. I just wanted a fucking donut. Mad as I was, I thought better of the bathrobe idea and decided I had better get dressed and start walking.

So far as I could tell, there were two universal truths that pertained to donut shops everywhere. One: all had been lit to such an excessive fluorescent brightness that it seemed like the terrifying herald of a nuclear event; and two: no matter how gleaming the glass, nor how neat the rows of freshly baked, i.e., fried, items, the rest of the shop appeared to be one dropped spoon or spilled coffee cup away from disintegrating into a heap of rubble. There wasn't anything especially forlorn about this particular donut shop, whose name happened to be Donut Madness. It was more that, a donut joint right smack in the inner city of this *particular* inner city meant that every single person coming in and out of the donut shop was forlorn.

"Are you at all acquainted with squalor?" I had read the J.D. Salinger story that inspired my name countless times. I analyzed the story and dissected the character of Esmé. I searched for clues, though I was never certain what I was searching for clues *of*. I looked up all the words that I didn't know in our dictionary. I looked up many words that I did know as well, such as the word "squalor." "Filth and misery," Webster's said. Brief and punchy, I thought. A vivid, clear, comprehensive picture painted in just two words. "Especially when being the result of poverty and neglect," Webster continued. Donut Madness. Nailed in four words. Filth. Misery. Poverty. Neglect.

The day that I first happened upon the Hangover Donut was one for the record books.

I was in such wretched shape that I staggered in, made my way toward the cash register and laid my head right down on the glass counter. With my head cradled in my arms, I moved my fuzzy eyes—very slowly—up and down the rows of an amazing array and variety of donuts. In reality, there may well have been fewer than a dozen different flavors, but in my condition, the display seemed overwhelming. The donut guy sidestepped over to where I rested, adjusted his triangular paper hat and said, "May I help you?" in the most polite and casual way imaginable. He even looked me in the eye. With no judgment. I slowly raised my right arm so my elbow rested while I proceeded to point with my index finger in the direction of the donut case. "Which one?" He said, moving his head this way and that to get a better sense of where I might be pointing. "This one?" he asked me. I moved my head back and forth a fraction of an inch; enough for him to know that I meant no; I used my thumb to point to the left, then to point down. Bless the man; he clearly knew better than to ask me which donut I wanted by saying the name of the flavor. Apparently Donut Madness had plenty of customers who wandered in in various circumstances that rendered them unable to read the fetching names of the flavors on the little signs. The donut man moved his own index finger to the left one donut, then down one row and said, "Ah. This one?" I gave him a thumbs up. He said, "Excellent choice. Truly an excellent donut."

Once I had managed to fish a five-dollar bill from my jeans, pay, leave a tip, pocket the change, and take the bag from the man, he adjusted his hat and said, "Thank you. Enjoy your excellent donut, and come back again."

It's hard to describe what I put in my mouth once safely outside. I took a bite, and…it was like someone had created a super dense, heavy dough that could soak up three or four times the usual amount of grease. One bite, and I felt as if every bit of my face below my nose must surely be covered with grease. It oozed down the sides of my mouth. It was then that I realized the donut itself seemed to weigh about a pound, which I figured was a half-pound of dough and a half pound of grease. Fried chicken meets funnel cakes. I took another bite and gazed at the donut in rapture while I chewed. Who invented this unexpected wonder? Two bites, and I began to believe that my entire day, my entire outlook on life and humanity and the possibility of a robust future were within my reach.

If I had been in less woeful condition than I was, I may have waxed sentimental for that Sunday in mid-fall when I first visited Donut Madness. Time had passed. Hangovers bruised far more than in the early days of my relationship with alcohol. Such lofty heights as belief in a robust future were much too high of a bar to set for the remaining scraps of this day. I was willing to settle for being somewhat awake, somewhat dressed (because at some point while I was walking to Donut Madness, a glance down toward the sidewalk revealed that I had, in fact, thrown my coat right on top of my pink bathrobe; it hadn't just been a thought), and somewhat in control of my fac—of my f-a-c-u-l-t-i-e-s for a few short hours before I gave up once and for all on this particular day of my life. I had pinned my hopes—possibly it's even fair to say that I had prayed—that I would get the donut guy who usually worked on Sundays. The wonderful man would reach for a Hangover Donut with his tissue-wrapped hand and have it in a bag on the counter by the time I made it from the front door to the cash register. I didn't need to utter a sound nor even point a finger. It wasn't his fault that the clang of the cash register was so brain piercing that it threatened my tenuous grasp, and he always said, "Thank you. Enjoy your excellent donut, and come back again."

Despite my best effort to nurse and savor that one cup of coffee so it would magically last forever, the contents continued to diminish as I continued to drink. I held the cup up to the street light as I approached the archway entrance closest to my dorm and grieved to see the shadowed evidence of one remaining inch. I was holding the dwindling warmth of the Styrofoam cup to my forehead when I saw. There sat Tom, on the wide steps leading to the entrance of my dorm and two other dorms as well. A very large cup of coffee and a brown bag from the donut shop kept him company. The smoke from his inevitable cigarette and the steam rising from the torn-back hole in the coffee cup's lid made magical swirls as they rose and vanished.

"Hey," I said.

"Hey," Tom said back.

"Were you just there? How could we possibly have missed each other?"

"Good question," Tom held the bag out toward me. "For you," he said.

"Has anyone ever eaten two of those things? I mean, ever?"

"Good question," he said, lowering the bag and holding up a full, steaming coffee cup. It may as well have been the Holy Grail. "This is also for you."

"Bless you," I said. I plunked down beside him on the steps and took the coffee. "How did you know, by the way?"

"I added two plus two. Someone said you seemed really pissed off after dinner last night. Someone else saw you getting cozy with a guy who pulled an unopened bottle of Southern Comfort from a bag. Nobody saw you today at brunch."

"I wasn't getting cozy with the guy. I was getting cozy with the bottle of Southern Comfort. Just so we're clear."

Tom laughed, in his minimalist way, just as he was exhaling a puff from his cigarette. Staccato bursts of smoke and steam lived their brief and glorious lives in front of us. He pointed his cigarette at the length of pink robe and laughed again. "Want to talk about it? Whatever happened yesterday?"

"No," I said. "Not hardly. No. And also, before we move on from the subject of things we're not talking about, please let us never mention the name of that particular brand of liquor again, ever."

Tom put his arm around me and squeezed my shoulder.

I drew deep from the warmth and creaminess of my coffee and found myself profoundly moved by the entire scene. The night sky, the cold air, the steaming cup, my old bathrobe, Tom and me on the stairs—I'm not sure what it was, but everything seemed to be in sharper focus while we sat there. "Tom Donahue, this may be the very nicest, sweetest, kindest thing that anyone has ever done for me." I raised my coffee cup in salute. "I mean it. You, waiting for me here on the steps, with the donut, the coffee…"

He didn't say anything. No need to.

I gently whacked my body against his as I said, "I'm still not having sex with you, though. Just so we're clear."

CHAPTER 32

THE ICY GRAY RELENTLESSNESS HAD DUG ITS CLAWS INTO ME. A constant murk loitered in my gut. Seven o'clock on a Thursday night. Early. A seemingly random time to take a shower, but I had drawn out dinner as long as I could with a lengthy sequence of cups of coffee, and I wasn't ready to face the evening—to decide whether I would gather folks to head to the bar, again again again, or possibly to study something. Which meant, by that point, to pretend to study something. I took showers at all kinds of haphazard times, when I needed to feel the potency of warmth that only immersion can bring. Growing up, I relied on baths. But there were no such things as bathtubs at college. Nor were there children. Nor dogs. There were all kinds of things that you never saw. They simply disappeared from one's landscape for a number of years.

I had worked up a bountiful cloud of steam. The shower's intense heat within the cold of the marble dormitory bathroom caused the column of steam to shoot toward the ceiling in a whirling frenzy. I closed my eyes and focused on the feeling of my fingertips massaging the shampoo through my scalp while the water fell on my abdomen and cascaded down my legs. With my eyes still closed, I turned around, leaned my head back and rinsed the shampoo from my hair, feeling the rivers of suds tumble down my back and pool around my feet.

When the shampoo had been fully rinsed, I rubbed the water from my eyes and opened them.

A pair of dark brown eyes—brown eyes on the face of a man—stared straight at me, framed by the fingertips of two hands.

The top of the man's head, encased in a ratty dark blue stocking cap, rose up from the partial wall that was opposite the wall of the shower head.

The eyes. My mind was filled by the eyes.

I froze. Paralyzed. Of all things, I found myself trying to figure out what in the world he was standing on, that he would be able to look over the *top* of the six-and-a half-foot shower wall.

He vanished.

Even with the noise of the shower water continuing to run, I felt as if a menacing silence was devouring me.

I don't know how long I stood there, frozen in the whirls of steam, before I turned around to face the other direction. And there he was. Part of his body—his entire body from his mid-torso up to the creepy stocking cap—was rising over the opposite shower wall. He was hoisting himself. He was trying to crawl over the top of the shower wall to get *inside* the stall with me.

I knew there was no one else around.

I knew there was only one reason why a man would be trying to trap me in a shower stall.

No one was ever around the dorm at that hour.

I wanted to scream. I wanted to scream so loud so loud so loud, my voice would rip right out of my chest and be gone, for days it would be gone. But there was no one to hear me. I figured the guy, the guy who had already become a giant head with giant sad dead eyes and a giant scruffy Afro stuffed into a ratty dusty stocking cap, dusty like he had been rolling around on the barren winter ground right before he, right before he… he was probably carrying—a gun, at least a knife. A gun or a knife. A thunderous or a silent end to my life, a hole blown through me or my skin hacked open.

From what I could see, he seemed huge. Six feet three, six feet four.

It just didn't seem like a good idea to scream.

In the few seconds I stood there, watching my blood drain out of my body and fuse with the shower water in my mind, I saw him out of the corner of my eye. That eye again. One eye this time. Looking at me. Looking through the sliver of space between the shower door and the door frame. The bulk of his body was directly behind the shower door. The giant sad dead eye.

It was instinct, like a reflex. With the full force of my weight, I pushed the shower door right into his face. Right into his fucking face. Fast thinker, he turned out to be. He shoved the door back toward me, and he ran. Like hell, he ran. When I rammed the shower door open again—naked and dripping and gulping for air—the bathroom's main entrance door still hung open from the force of his push, and I caught a glimpse of him rounding the first turn, hurtling down the five flights of stairs between him and the freshman quadrangle gate and the anonymity of the night. Winter black bleak night in the seedy downtown where his dead eyes and his tattered stocking cap would not stand out one bit.

I stood in the bathroom, the shower still running, shivering head to toe. My teeth chattered. My body, bright pink from the scorching water, felt like it had no blood in it at all, as if the terror had leached it right out of my skin. At some point I turned off the water but felt swallowed by the silence, terrified by the absence of the sound. I turned the shower back on, focused hard on the sound of the stream, the warmth of the water, so I could hold them inside of me, then turned the handle off again.

I wrapped myself in my towel and looked at my reflection in the mirror above the perfectly polished sinks. I needed to see myself. I needed to make sure that I was still there. Though I had seen the man with the huge, bloodshot brown eyes bolting down the stairs after he tore out of the bathroom, I did not trust what I had seen. I stayed in the bathroom for a long time, a long long time. Tentatively, slowly, I cracked the bathroom door a hair and looked around for any sign that he might still be close.

Nothing. The worn marble of the common area on the fourth-floor landing, the old staircase, four closed doors. Wait, not all of the doors were closed. The door to my own dorm room was ajar.

I had left it closed.

I was certain of this.

My door stood open a few inches. Two, maybe three. No light came from inside my room. I reminded myself again that I had seen the guy tearing down the stairs. Even in the flash of time that the bathroom door was open, I saw him round the bend on the landing. Mom loved the expression "bat out of hell." He was moving like the proverbial bat from the evil stinking putrid world of hell. I convinced myself there was no way this guy would have reversed direction, come back up the stairs, and lay hiding and waiting for me in my room. Right?

Right?

I called out into the empty space, "Carrie?"

I waited a time and called out again, louder this time, "Hey, Carrie?"

Nothing. The slight echo of my own voice bounced around the stairwell. The inscrutable faces of the solid, closed doors faced me. And still, the door to my own room, open, waiting for me.

I pushed my room door so hard that it crashed against the wall and made a thunderous noise, then I raced around and turned on every single light in the entire suite, then went straight to my closet and put on my crazy pink bathrobe. My security, my blankie. Ugly, overly-girly, too pink, so many things all wrong about it. But Mom had made it. She'd gotten out her old sewing machine and worked on it in secret when I wasn't around and surprised me with it years earlier. I treasured it. Beyond all reason, I treasured it. I wrapped myself within its rough, cheap-towel envelope and pulled the collar up around my face. The robe held me. It kept me alive. It kept me safe. Safe for the tears to come, finally, for the tears to come.

Not all the tears, though. I needed to call the campus police. I needed to get through that ordeal first.

I tried to compress my neck so my head could disappear entirely within the robe's collar. As I did this, I noticed something. The cupboard door above my desk was open. I never left it open. Never.

I didn't keep much in that cupboard. Clean underwear, if there was any. A pile of unmatched socks. And one more thing, an important thing—a trashy little jewel box with ornate, peeling gold sides and a glass top. The bottom of the box was lined with an ivory velvet cushion. I had laid out my four special rings on that velvet cushion when I first unpacked my things back in the fall, and I chose one of them to wear each day. One of the four rings was on my finger. The other three rings were gone.

Oh my god ohmygod. The bastard, the bastard, *the bastard!* He'd robbed me! Before he came into the fucking shower, he'd fucking robbed me!

One had been my grandmother's engagement ring. One, my aunt brought back from the only real vacation she had ever been able to take. The black star sapphire, my mother had given me for my high school graduation.

Loneliness tore through me. I rested my forehead against the window frame and looked out at the winter night.

A tie to a grandmother I had never met. A tie to an aunt

who had scrimped and saved to take one real vacation in her whole life. A tie to my mom. The black star sapphire ring was so inexpensive that the gold had already begun to discolor. The cheap, discolored ring that I could not have loved one iota more.

Gone. Stolen. Taken from me no less than if they had been pieces of my soul. Things of no value to anyone else. But for me, holes left. More holes.

I made my way over to the phone, took deep breaths and tried to steady my trembling as I dialed the number for the campus police. The woman asked me a couple of quick questions and decided this was a matter for the city police. The campus police would call them for me, she said. The city officers would come straight to my room, she said. The person on the phone assured me that everyone would take this matter quite seriously and the police would be there soon. She sounded bored, completely uninterested.

The cops did come soon. I barely had time to toss on some clothes from the floor of my closet, my hair still soaking wet and an uncombed, tangled mess when the knock came.

CHAPTER 33

TWO MIDDLE-AGED WHITE COPS, NOT EVEN WEARING COATS in the dead of winter, ambled into my dorm suite looking both professional and completely indifferent. Each carried a cup of coffee from Donut Madness. Small fucking world. The smell of the coffee was heaven, a waft of such pure and simple bliss that I felt tears well in my eyes. I had no idea why.

"Evening, miss," the shorter one said, "We hear you had some trouble."

"Yeah, I…"

"Hold it, miss," the other officer interrupted me to say. "I want to make sure I get all of this down." He reached into his pocket and pulled out the tiniest little notebook I'd ever seen then reached into a different pocket and retrieved a comically short pencil stub. The three of us stood silently while the policeman shuffled through the teeny notebook to find a blank page. Everything shifted and slid into the surreal. Was this really happening? The whole thing—starting with a *guy* in the *women's bathroom* on the *fourth-floor walk-up* who was *trying to…trying to….* I wanted to run into my bedroom and check my jewelry box again, see for myself that the rings were gone, that they were really gone and that all of this had actually happened and that there really were two fucking weird ass cops standing in the fireplace room ready to make notes with a kindergarten pencil in a microscopic notebook. When the police guy found a blank page, he said aloud as he started to write, "Ok. February 7, nineteen seventy-four—" at which point the pencil tip broke off and flew toward me. "Ah, crap, that was my very last pencil. You got another one on you, Al?"

"Not me, buddy. You're the note guy," Other Cop Al said.

As if I were sleepwalking, I reached over to grab one of the gazillion pens, pencils, markers, highlighters, etc., etc., etc., that Carrie and I had lying around everywhere. Holding the pen out to the cop, I saw the ring on my finger. My one remaining ring. A small ruby in a plain gold setting, the birthstone I shared with my grandmother.

"He took my rings," I said. "He stole them."

"What?" The policeman said, "Hey, sorry, Miss, but I only use pencils. Pens make a mess of the notes. If you have to cross stuff out."

"Oh," I said. "Sorry." I turned away to switch out the pen for a pencil and thought I saw a little smile on Al's face when I turned back around. Perhaps it was sympathetic, but I did not feel certain.

Notetaking Cop had his eyebrows raised, like something was especially interesting, or maybe amusing. He straightened up his face and said, "You were saying? Something about rings?"

"The guy," I said. "The same guy who was…in the bathroom with me. He must have been in my room first. In here. He stole three of my rings from in there." I pointed behind me, toward my bedroom, and the cops dutifully turned their heads.

"Hey, hold it. Hold up a minute. Rings you say?"

"Yes!" I said. In a voice that emerged louder and more tremulous than I expected.

"Al," the notetaking cop said, "Had to be that guy. That *guy!*"

"Oh, that *guy,*" Al said, pointing his finger as if it were an exclamation mark.

"Was this man black, miss? Real tall?"

"Yes," I said. "*Yes.*"

"We saw him. On our way over here. Walking north on Elm when we got out of our car. Looked like he was high as a kite, so we talked to him, you know? Asked him if he was all right and where he was going, and he goes to scratch his nose, and he's got, like, rings on all of his fingers. Rings! Looked kinda expensive and kinda like girl rings, too, so I asked him, I says, 'Hey nice rings, where'd you get the nice rings?' And he says…I don't know what he says, but hey, guy's walking down the street, and we were on our way here… How do we know where he got the rings, right? But I'm thinking, I'm thinking now, that must have been your guy."

I just stood there.

"I actually said to Al, I said to him when we were walking away, I said, 'Al, one of those rings looked pretty nice, right?'"

I snapped into focus when he said that. Out of the numb, sleepwalking, surreal emotionless detachment I'd been in since the cops knocked on my door. Since I looked into the jewel box and saw the empty velvet pillow. Since I looked in the bathroom mirror to make sure I was really there. Since I saw two sad dead eyes that wanted to hurt me.

I locked onto Notetaking Cop's eyes, and I looked hard, and I saw it.

He hated me.

He had been unfailingly polite, but nonetheless.

I was the enemy.

I was one of the sheltered, privileged rich kids who went to That School.

I wanted to scream. I wanted to sob. I wanted to tell them every single thing that I felt from the moment I first saw the dead eyes and the ratty stocking cap and I wanted to talk forever and not skip any of it, I wanted them to know exactly what it was like to have the the the pictures in my head the gun that would blast a hole clear through my body a cartoon hole that you could see right through or the knife that would open my skin like a zipper had been pulled and the blood the blood all the blood and wondering when would he rape me when would he rape me when would it happen to me would it be before he hurt me or after when would my life change forever in a shower stall a shower stall not a hundred feet from my bedroom window where frozen vomit spilled down an ivy-covered stone wall at this crazy awful evil school. And I wanted to say, maybe most of all I wanted to say, no no no I am not one of them! I am not one of them I am NOT. I am one of you! One of you just like you! I grew up poor and we had nothing! Nothing! my mother worked her butt off and please please don't think that I am one of them. *I am here on scholarship!!*

Notetaker turned to Al and said, "You got a tissue on you?"

I didn't know that I had been crying until I saw the long, gooey stream that must have been coming from my nose. Hanging in mid-air, suspended, a thin thread reaching toward the floor. I was mortified, and I wiped the great stream with my bathrobe collar, which made me far more mortified.

Notetaker said, "Hey, miss? Do you have a friend you might want to call? Someone to come over and stay with you for a while?" I nodded. "How about if you call them up while we're still here? Do you want to do that? Call now?"

"No, that's ok," I said. "I'll wait."

Notetaker handed back my pencil and crammed the notebook into his pocket. "Don't you worry about a thing," he said. "We're gonna get this guy. We will definitely get him."

It wasn't until after they left that I realized they had not written down a single thing.

CHAPTER 34

I'D NEVER STOLEN ANYTHING IN MY ENTIRE LIFE. NOT EVEN when so many of the girls I knew back in Clarion, Pennsylvania, were pocketing a lipstick here, a jar of nail polish there, and proudly recounting their heroic tales of brave and valorous theft while they nibbled on skimpy lunches in the school cafeteria. But six months into the school year, my body had started to feel different. Foreign and wobbly. Like my head had gained an enormous amount of weight and a blind force was pulling my fingertips toward the ground all the time. Plus, even though I considered myself an amateur, recreational smoker, I had recently started buying my own packs and was horrified to find myself panting by the time I hit the final set of stairs to my dorm room. I figured that I needed to find some way to move my body around more than just having the occasional non-committal sex and slogging through slush to and from the rare classes I still attended.

I signed up for a tour of the school's "athletic facility" and listened to a particularly zealous undergrad rattle on about various physical challenges that one could attack with the same intensity and vigor that we undoubtedly approached our academics. Once inside the "athletic facility" itself, I felt like

I had been thrust into a Brobdingnagian version of my high school gym, everything exploded to a ridiculous scale—the height of the ceilings, the echoing thumps, skidding shoes and overlapping shouts coming from distant basketball courts, the smell of effusions from scores of human bodies that were continually being wrestled by chemical eradicators.

And then. The pool. When we wandered into the warm, humid room that enclosed the giant-est swimming pool I had ever seen, I wanted to fall on my knees in gratitude for the life-giving, fecund warmth that surrounded me. The gentle ripple sounds that the oceanic amount of water made against the sides of the pool. The same beautiful old ochre tile that lined the Squirrel Hill Tunnel in Pittsburgh. I wanted to stay forever and never, ever leave.

And the best part of all was that this outsized pool was completely empty. Of people, I mean. Nearly empty, at any rate. There was one, only one, person who was actually swimming. One other guy stood along the side in a dry bathing suit demonstrating that it was, in fact, possible to putter while standing in one place. He fiddled with his goggle strap, adjusted the waistband of his suit, swung his arms in giant circles, then repeated the series. The whole time I stood there in my awkward euphoric state, it remained unclear whether he might eventually swim, or whether he had swum so long ago that his swimsuit had dried entirely, or whether his sole intention was to stand along the pool's edge and putter. A lifeguard perched in an official-looking chair. I supposed he already knew that nobody actually swam. He had come prepared. He looked up from his book, calculus I think it was, infrequently and for less than a full second each time.

It was warm. It was devoid of other humans. It had the comforting sound of lapping water and the Squirrel Hill Tunnel tiles. No matter that I had not swum in years. No matter that the only time I had *ever* actually swum from one end of a swimming pool to the other end was for the final swim test of the one and only swim class I had ever taken. And at that moment, the instructor, bless her heart, acted entirely calm as I sputtered and gasped my way through that one interminable length. She walked along the edge right next to me the whole time, even though I had been a total wiseass cut-up to Red Cross Swim Instructor Mary Pickle for the entire class. When I dragged my humbled ass out of the pool at the end of my sole length, Mary Pickle extended her hand for me to shake then changed her mind and gave me a genuine bear hug. I do believe she was quite relieved that I had survived. Also relieved that she could certify that I had officially passed the course and would not need to return for another go-round in her pool. It wasn't like I'd had a different, or especially good, relationship with swimming in all the years after that, either. None of that reality mattered, however, so ardent was my desire to be in that pool. I had already become convinced that this body of water was my own personal Lourdes. My sins would be washed away, my wounds healed, and the sickness that held a death grip on my soul would unclench its ghastly rotting teeth and wash away.

All I needed was a bathing suit.

Which I did not have.

The one thing that could possibly have motivated me to leave the promise of the pool's restorative powers was the need to acquire a swimsuit so I could return. I made a beeline to the school's bookstore, which sold every possible thing a student might ever need. Half of one floor was devoted to books; the remaining acreage held a treasure trove of spirit wear, posters, toiletries, lab equipment, snacks, small appliances, 623 different sizes of batteries, and—I never doubted—Speedo swimsuits for a would-be lap-swimming student such as myself.

I was right. They had two different colors of the same style in my size—solid navy blue or a brashly bold red, white and blue pattern called "Union Jack." I held those two boxes and studied them as if the swimsuit decision had the power to direct the future course of my entire life. Because the actual swimsuit showed through a windowpane on the box's front side, it was quite a while before I turned the boxes over to view the back side. My sole intention was to waste a little more time while I pondered the solemn decision about color, and I thought I may as well read the words on the flip side of the box that some marketing guy had been handsomely paid to pen.

On the bottom right corner of the back side, there was the unobtrusive little price sticker—a price that was so far above any amount I could have imagined that I didn't know what in the world to do. I felt rooted to the drab linoleum tile floor, unable to budge, the weighty feeling of my fingertips being pulled toward the floor upon me once again. I didn't need to check my wallet or rifle my pockets to know that I had nowhere near that kind of money. No way I would hit up friends for that amount, either. And even if I could stand to wait for the soothing redemption I believed the pool offered me, there was no chance I would ask Mom to send me any more cash. I knew how much she had tightened her belt by this time. There were no more notches for her to tighten.

Stealing was my only option. I had to. Fuck trying to choose which color, fuck that. Fuck Speedo for charging so absurdly much for an infinitesimal amount of fabric—I was going to take them both. With a quick look around, I stuffed Royal Navy into one side of my coat and Union Jack into the other, pulled my coat's belt tight and took my time getting out of there, pretending to be casual while I perused gym shorts, socks, all kinds of crap. I inspected each article like I had all the time in the world, and I was a discerning, careful shopper. After a detailed inspection, I made an expression of subtle disapproval, as if I had determined that the item's quality was not quite the caliber I sought. After I had done this a bunch of times, I put my hands in my pockets and sauntered toward the front door with my head held high.

The second my foot crossed the threshold, the late winter air slapped me in the face. I may have gasped. I quickly adjusted the stolen goods for the walk home and forced myself to put one foot in front of the other.

"Hey." A man's voice came from just behind my left shoulder. Oh no. No no no. No way I could have been caught. Plus, the voice sounded calm, not like someone about to apprehend a criminal. I continued to play my chosen role, still acting the part of the casual, poised undergrad, and I said, "Hey," while I was still in the process of turning toward the voice.

"Hey," the guy said again. Young guy. Street guy. Not a student. Oh, shit.

Oh, shit. I turned back around without saying anything more and quickened my pace. I was pretty sure the guy was following me.

"Hey," he said for the third time. "Have a cup of coffee with me. How about it?"

I couldn't figure out what to do, whether to ignore him or tell him to go away and it was not my first time being followed in this wretched town at this wretched school and I was tired of it, tired of all of it, tired to my frozen bones and all I had wanted to do was get a swimsuit so I could float in a warm sea of pure embracing water, and now this guy, this asshole guy was following me and asking me if I wanted to get a cup of coffee with him, and no I didn't want to get a cup of coffee with him, I couldn't believe it, I couldn't fucking believe it.

I stopped in my tracks and turned around to confront him. He had a cup in his hand. A coffee cup. From Donut Madness. It was as if an electric zap of terror hit me right in the center of my forehead. I could feel my eyes darting crazily around the street scene in a desperate attempt to let the remaining daylight, the people on the sidewalk, the heavy traffic reassure me that I was safe, that I would be OK, because I knew that I wasn't OK, I wasn't OK at all.

CHAPTER 35

I DID A LITTLE PIROUETTE AND TOOK OFF IN A NEAR-RUN, pressing my hands against the front of my coat so the Speedo boxes wouldn't tumble out. I knew it must look like I was clutching my own boobs as I clipped down the sidewalk, and people on all sides stared openly, no attempts to hide their gawking whatsoever. I felt a heavy tear plop out and race down my cheek. I shifted my death grip on the swimsuit boxes, and with the heel of my palm, I pushed the tear back up my cheek and into my eye. Then I pressed against my eyelid to hold it in.

Everything was chasing me. I was terrified to turn around, certain that I would see a whole world of people and things amassing and following me: the guy, Dr. David Ackerman, Donut Madness coffee cups, Southern Comfort, vomit-laden ivy, the shower man flashing my rings at me and laughing, the cops waving teeny pencil stubs and slapping each other on the back.

Everything got dark around the edges. My field of vision narrowed to a pinpoint of watery daylight that aimed directly at the entrance gate of the freshman quad. I made a mad dash for it, passed through the archway and—with the slight residue of sanity that remained—determined that I needed to hide my true identity and actual home location by flimflamming. Boobs still in hand, I traversed the width of the quad and bolted into the Tom and Tommy entryway. I immediately reversed course, upchucked and retched into the bushes for a while, then returned to sit in the stairwell.

Little me curled in a ball, alone alone alone at the bottom of a stairwell, running my fingers back and forth, running them along icy frozen freezing veiny veined marble. More than a thousand freshman circled at a distance, five thousand undergrads, six thousand grad students intertwined and interwoven and circling in stony, mocking silence.

A door opens, and Montgomery Treadwell III emerges like an actor like a fucking actor in a play where the main character is in hell, she is in hell, and Montgomery Treadwell III is dressed in his monogrammed robe and leather scuff slippers and his monogrammed towel is draped perfectly over the crook of his arm, and he looks down at me, in every possible way he looks down at me and he says, "Esmé, are you all right?" while he comes not one step not one inch closer, it's like he's picked up the scent of madness and he's keeping his distance, I've become a thing that he needs to keep his distance from, and I say "Montgomery, I need to use your phone." And I remember to say please even though I don't wait for his answer, I don't wait I jump up and grab my boobs/stolen Speedos and blow right past him and pick up his room phone from the very same place that my room phone is in my room, and I dial the office number for Dr. McClelland, and the second the phone picks up and I hear that practiced

practiced practiced professional voice, I break down into hysterical, racking sobs and I say, "Mom, you should have told me. You should have told me the truth."

SPRING
2 0 2 0

"This is the squalid, or moving, part of the story."

—J.D. Salinger
"For Esmé—with Love and Squalor"

CHAPTER 36

I CALL HER THE OLD GIRL. "GOOD MORNING, OLD GIRL," I say to my dog each morning as I rub her ears and kiss the top of her head. I inhale the scent of her as I do, at the place where the bone protrudes from the back of her skull and where her fur is the fuzziest downiest remnant of her puppyhood. "You smell just like yourself," I say.

It was a hard thing to ask of her, the magnitude of such a major move at this point in her life. Plagued by joint problems from an early age, the Old Girl's elbows have eroded in some places and sprouted the unwanted growth of severe arthritis in other places. Her walk has slowed. Her limp is often pronounced. It can be painful to watch, and sometimes I need to look away so she will not see me cry.

Her spirit remains undaunted. Each day, I ask her if she wants to see "the ducks," our catch-all term for the sundry waterfowl that populate the lakefront. I am asking if she is feeling well enough to make the two-block journey to the lake. After we have navigated our way down the first hallway to the elevator to the service lobby through the two fire doors, and we emerge—finally—into the outside world, I ask her about the ducks. Some days, she does a couple of tiny hops to indicate that her answer is yes. She has figured out that, on the downward incline of the ramp that leads to the tunnel that leads to the lakefront, i.e., to the ducks, gravity will do enough of the work that she can feel as if she is running. It thrills her; the lift in her entire being shines out. She is able to run, just as she did for so many years in her youth.

But there are days when the distance to the lake is too great. On these days, there are no little hops. With her feet planted squarely on the ground, she turns her head in the opposite direction, away from the lake, telling me that walking around the block is all she can manage.

As we walk down our block on this particular morning, the Old Girl picks up her pace when we near the corner. She strains at the leash, which is essentially unheard of since it causes her pain. A vicious tirade spontaneously combusts in my head, a diatribe against thoughtless reckless destructive urbanites who wantonly toss large amounts of their uneaten food—and all its accompanying plates, utensils, ketchup packages, plastic bags and a mind-boggling array of materials that will remain on the planet long after all life forms have vanished, except perhaps cockroaches—right on the street when they have decided they've finished eating. I wonder, then, if the Old Girl's decision to walk around the block has been based entirely on there being a better (in her mind) class of garbage available at infinite points along the way. I have learned that she pulls on the leash only when she has caught the scent of a particularly fine treasure of dumped rubbish; hence, my internal rant against the trash who tossed the trash.

I turn my own internal corner, I become enraged with *her,* the beloved dog herself, for being an *animal,* a lowly creature who strains and pulls toward her own possible destruction by ingesting God-knows-what.

But, no.

A man sits in the street. An older man, my age. He is near the curb, but he's in the street nonetheless. He glances from side to side, his mouth slightly open, his expression blank. He attempts to stand. I can't tell if he's unable to stand, or if he has changed his mind and decided not to try after all. He sits again, legs splayed at odd angles. A young woman stands on the sidewalk facing him, about ten feet away. She holds her phone out in front of her, as if she is thinking she may take a picture. She looks at me. "I've called 9-1-1," she says. "I've already called them."

A man stands at a careful distance. He, too, holds his phone up. "I called them, too. They are on their way."

The Old Girl goes to the edge of the street, as close as she can get to the man without going into the street itself, and she lies down. She drapes her paws over the edge of the curb.

A car comes screeching to a halt. Two doors slam. People get out from either side, leaving their car right where they stopped, mid-lane. Two phones are held aloft, but the people stay where they are, hovered next to their car doors. They move no closer. "We got him!" the man says. He is panting. "We chased him down…"

"…We got his plate numbers…" the woman says.

"…And we called it in. They got him."

"…The cops, he means. They already got the guy."

"I got a *picture* of his plates! His damn plates! I got a picture!"

I look to the young woman, the first one who spoke to me, as if she can magically provide all the answers.

"Hit and run," she says to me. "Car driving crazy fast hit this guy here (she points to the older man in the street) and drove away. Drove right away, didn't even slow down."

"We got the son of a bitch!" the man yells from his position at the door of his car, his voice both tremulous and triumphant. He is still panting. Sweat covers his brow, and he wipes it away with his hand.

The older man looks at me. Even with his mask, I can see that he is in pain. I take a hesitant step toward him. The young woman holds her hand out as if to stop me and says, "They're on their way. They should be here soon."

There is visible pain in the man's eyes. Confusion. Disorientation. But mostly pain.

I take another step closer to him. "Do you know what happened to you?" I ask him.

"Yes," he says, "I was hit. I was hit by a car."

Again the man attempts to stand. He wobbles and winces audibly.

"Don't try to stand," I say to him, but he is already trying again. I think that he must be in shock. I think that he doesn't know exactly what he's doing. And suddenly it doesn't matter. It doesn't matter because there is a human being in front of me, a human being who is injured and in pain and in shock and confused and no one will go near him, no one will help him, and I know that I'm not supposed to, I know that we are all supposed to obey the rules, that all of our futures depend on obeying the rules, and I know all of that and yet I step off the curb and I crouch down to speak to the man, but he reaches out his hand, it's instinct, I can see that he's not thinking, he's reaching out his hand in blind instinct and pain.

He grabs my arm with his hand, and I hesitate for less than a second before I cover his hand with my own, and I hold on. "Don't try to stand," I say. "If you're hurt, you may injure yourself more. Let's wait until the paramedics get here, OK?"

It has been a long time since I have heard my own Mother Voice, the maternal tone that emerged whenever a child needed a calm, confident, reassuring parent figure. A nether me that seemed to summon itself without my knowledge. "I'll stay right here with you. I'll stay until they get here."

The man looks into my eyes. He looks into them as if focusing on my eyes can save his life. "Thank you," he says.

"Frank?!" A woman's voice pierces the scene, and the man and I look up. A large woman in a bright red coat shields her eyes from a sun which has not shown itself today and calls out again, "Is that you, Frank?"

The man looks at me and nods his head. "Yes, that's me," he says.

"Yes, it's him," I shout to her. "He was hit by a car. The paramedics are on their way."

The young woman and the young man, still in their original positions, wave their phones in the air to confirm my story.

"Hit and run. We got the bastard!" says the man standing by his car. He waves his phone.

"Well. Oĸ," says the large woman in the red coat. She shuffles her weight from one foot to the other and says, "Oĸ, then." She takes a few steps away from us, turns and says, "I'll check on you later, I guess."

Frank re-arranges himself on the pavement and holds his arm up toward me, his other arm, not the one whose hand still clutches my own. "It hurts," he says. "It hurt a little bit before, but now it's starting to hurt more."

I look at the arm and nod to Frank. Even through his sleeve, I can tell. "It's broken," I say in the calm Mother Voice. "They'll fix that right up, and they'll check every bit of you." He looks so bewildered, lost, adrift that I say, "Does your head hurt, Frank? Did you hit your head at all?"

"You're touching me," Frank says. He looks at my hand, then again into my eyes. He doesn't say more. But I understand from his eyes, his voice, how long it has been since anyone has touched him.

CHAPTER 37

I HAD SEEN ALL THIS BEFORE. THE PAIN, THE FEAR, THE haunted, desolate isolation.

After the shower, the stolen bathing suit, after my total breakdown in front of Montgomery Treadwell III while I spewed at my mother, I threw a few things into a duffle and walked to the downtown bus station with no destination in mind. I stood in the terminal amidst a surprising crowd of people considering the small size of the city. I stared at the display board where the scheduled times of what seemed like a million buses changed every few seconds with a metallic click that announced the flip of the names and numbers.

The name of a particular city caught my eye: Falmouth. A town in Massachusetts that I knew of. Home of Woods Hole, a world-famous oceanographic institute. I knew about it from my high school friend Doug, who spoke about the place in rapturous tones and wedged tidbits of info about it into everyday conversations with laudable frequency. An oceanside hamlet at the tip of Massachusetts, with nothing much there and no population to speak of, at the bitter end of winter. Staring up at that schedule board, I was pretty sure that translated into: deserted. Devoid of other human beings. Empty of the exact things that could do even more damage to me. I envisioned a gigantic version of the swimming pool that had so thoroughly captured my fancy not long before, but with boundless vistas of the salty birthplace of all life, complete with crashing waves and cranky seagulls and a winter's worth of detritus strewn across the shore. In every way perfect, it seemed to me.

The bus was blessedly empty, so I didn't need to stare menacingly at anyone who even considered sitting in the seat next to me. The trip itself made no impression, not the quaint and charming small towns, not the squalid, heart-rendingly-past-their-heyday industrial-wasteland towns. I needed to be away—away from the college and the town and everything that I mentally rolled together and pictured as a giant ball of rot that shrank, smaller and smaller with each second that I did nothing but sit on the bus.

A person at the Falmouth, Massachusetts, bus stop told me that Woods Hole was a little less than four miles. It didn't occur to me until right then that I hadn't really planned this whole thing very well. I hadn't planned it at all. The person was genuinely helpful and gave me a lot of information. She told me that it would be an extra mile in each direction to get to the ocean, seeing as how the bus depot was in the exact middle of the landmass, with Buzzards Bay a mile in one direction and Vineyard Sound a mile in the other. Two more miles added to my already four-mile walk didn't seem worth it, seeing as how I'd have to say "Hi there, Ocean," then retrace my steps to get back to Woods Hole Road, the conveniently-named route that conveniently ran the entire way to my destination, albeit straight through the center of the isthmus or peninsula or whatever it was. No water in sight, in other words, for the entire walk.

I thought I must be getting pretty close to Woods Hole when I passed the Buckminster Fuller geodesic dome (I was too far gone to have even a whit of curiosity) and the Sands of Time Inn (the cloying cliché caused me physical pain). I rounded a turn on the road, and unexpectedly, the ocean-front soared into view. I had no way to know that Woods Hole Road had been wending its way toward the water while I traversed deep woods. It seemed like magic, divine magic.

With that bright, thin light of the dwindling afternoon at the cusp between winter and spring, the vast coastline before me looked like a slightly overexposed photograph. Like I was viewing my own faded memory from a later, future time. It took my breath away and thrilled me and filled me with a profound sense of calm. I figured I could see at least a mile of open beachfront, perhaps much more, and there was not one single other human being anywhere in sight.

"Hi," I said to the young woman. She was sitting behind a desk at the first building I found with an unlocked front door. I had tried many. "Hey, I hope you can help me." She smiled, set aside a notebook where it looked like she was scribbling, rubbed her hands together as if she were either freezing or terribly excited to be of service, and said, "What can I do for you?"

"Well, I wanted to see the place. If that's possible. My cousin Doug has been talking about Woods Hole forever, and he's coming here this summer for some workshop or class or something." I surprised myself at how easily and naturally the lies tumbled out of my mouth. Not that it really mattered whether Doug was my cousin. Nor did it matter whether the real-life Doug, or the fake cousin Doug, might be taking any sort of a class there. What did matter was that I could invent alternative realities with such frightening ease. "So…I thought I'd just hop on the bus, you know, from my college, and have a little break and check it out." A quick look around revealed absolutely nothing. Not a single sign of anyone else.

"Oh, well, how nice. I'm afraid there's not very much happening here at this time of the year," she said. "Not things that you can *see*, anyway."

"There are invisible things going on?" I asked. If it had been a different time, I might have said that same line with irony and been secretly impressed with my own wit. But at this particular time, I was incapable of doing anything other than taking the poor young woman at face value. I had asked the question with complete sincerity.

"No, no," she said. "I meant that you can't really *see* the research that people are doing. Everyone's either out in the field, i.e., the ocean, or they're at the computers."

I was charmed that she'd said "i.e.," out loud in a sentence, and I forgave her if she had, in fact, been trying to mess with me by suggesting that invisible work was being conducted all around us. "I see," I said. Without irony. "It does seem pretty empty."

She cackled in what seemed like a very strange way, but I

figured I wasn't the best judge of what was strange and what wasn't right then. "Yes. Pretty empty is entirely correct," she said, then rubbed her hands together again.

"I was thinking there would be places to stay right around here, but I haven't seen much."

She sat up straighter in her chair and perked up noticeably. "Oh, well, there's the Woods Hole Inn—just down the road— but you could stay right here, if you want. If you're a student, like you said, I can let you stay in one of our dormitories for a very small fee. You know, a dorm room like your cousin will be staying in this summer. Three dollars a night, in point of fact."

"Oh, wow, that's great," I said. I flashed my student ID and handed over three bucks in exchange for a lone key and a lengthy set of directions that involved a lot of gesturing and pointing.

Eventually I found the dorm building that was nothing like the Gothic structures at my college, any one of which could easily be mistaken for a cathedral or a monastery. These dorms had all the charm of post-war elementary schools—generic institutional designs whose points of pride were gleaming linoleum and hollow-core woodwork. When I put my key into the lock of my very own dorm room, I heard a faint flutter of activity close by. The door of the dorm room right next to mine burst open, and a small, bespectacled middle-aged man flew out and rushed toward me. He reached his arms out as if he intended to embrace me and made a guttural, animal-like sound.

I had a few seconds of unmitigated, unbridled, unrestrained

terror. But then I looked at his face, and in his eyes, I saw such unmitigated, unbridled, unrestrained pain that my own fear vaporized.

One of his hands reached me and touched my arm before he quickly withdrew it and flinched. "Oh, my God," he said. "I am so sorry. Oh, my God."

I couldn't figure out a response that seemed appropriate for this particular circumstance, so I simply said, "Hi."

"Oh, you must think I'm a *lunatic.* I've been here all winter by myself. Research. By myself. I haven't seen another…person…for a long time."

He didn't need to say anything, really. I had seen it in his eyes. He was not crazy. He was devoid of the modicum of human connection that we all need. In other words, he was lonely. In other words, he was my brethren.

"It's okay," I said to the man. "Really." I could see in his face that he was rattled and ashamed. I smiled and tried to indicate by my demeanor that I understood. I felt sad that the man had been humiliated and abased by his loneliness. I wanted badly to think of something I could say, but he hastily re-entered his room and closed the door behind him.

Once inside my own room, I found that having a new set of walls surrounding me, blue-gray paint rather than bright white, an unfamiliar bed where everything was different—the firmness of the pillow, the slippery feel of the synthetic sheets, the softness of the mattress—seemed both wildly exotic and profoundly comforting. It freed something in me. I slept a sound and dreamless sleep that night.

The next morning, armed with the largest cup of coffee I could carry, I puttered and meandered, examining the exteriors of a number of locked buildings. After a while, I wandered over to the oceanfront and kicked at various relics of the weather and tides. By the time the sun reached its highest point, the morning wind calmed, and the earth itself seemed to rise in exultation at the sun's muscular warmth.

The date on the calendar be damned, I was convinced that if I could find just the right spot, protected and sheltered just enough from the elements, I imagined that I could lie on the beach and bask in the sun's strength—wearing the purloined navy blue Speedo that I had tossed in my backpack, against all odds of having any use for it. I located such a spot, burrowed a little trough in the dirt-colored sand, and surrendered myself to the warm rays I fervently hoped would exorcise any and all remaining dung and rot and muck and vomit and toxin and bile and the sum total of foulness that I carried.

I awoke in the exact same position in the exact same spot three hours later. I had no idea it had been that long, not until I got back to my dorm room and saw a clock, though I had already noted the fact that my skin felt as if every bit of moisture had been sucked through my pores. An hour later, I knew I had a fever. My body turned pink and then red. Chills ran through me like electric shocks. My fever climbed higher still, and my ears rang with a continual, loud whine.

I have no recollection of how I got to the bus station. Perhaps someone, perhaps the woman at the desk, gave me a ride. I can't imagine how I could possibly have walked the four miles, considering the condition I was in, but I don't remember. I do remember pausing outside of the lonely man's door one final time as I was leaving. Though the doors of our rooms were less than twenty feet apart, I had not seen him again, nor had I heard a single sound. A couple of times, I put my ear to our adjoining wall. I had become worried about him, fearing that his shame had driven him deeper into whatever hell he inhabited. He had joined ranks with the engineers, Rob, Mark and the assorted others whose lonely pain touched something in me—an intense wish to protect them, to shelter them from any further hurt.

Despite the roar in my ears, I put my ear to his door, wishing for some sign of life to come from his room, some scrap of hope I could find that he might yet come through with all of his faculties intact.

CHAPTER 38

THE SUM TOTAL OF THAT ENTIRE INTERVAL—THE INTRICATE mixture of *everything* I'd experienced from the time I threw a few pairs of clean underwear into a pack in my dorm room until I found myself on the bus traveling the reverse course back to the loathsome college—inhabited me in a single instant as I crouched in the street with Frank.

The bespeckled man rushing out of his room, the despair and empty loneliness, the impassioned impulse for one life to connect with another. That is what I saw in Frank's eyes.

"I'll stay right here with you," I said to him again. The Old Girl had not moved a bit since she first lay down. It was not treasured garbage that she had strained at the leash to reach, it was Frank. "You'll be in good hands. The closest hospital is a very fine one. You'll be well taken care of." I was blithering, really. My words were essentially meaningless, just pleasant sounds to offer Frank something to focus on, something to anchor him.

The paramedics immediately rankled me with their officiousness, making a show of snapping on their sterile gloves and readjusting their masks before they came near enough to speak. Their leader was a giant of a man—tall and brawny and chiseled—who was so obviously impressed with his own fine attributes that I wanted to slap him.

In fairness, they probably were not officious, merely efficient, and my pique had to do with their interrupting a moment of human tenderness. As if he were thinking the same thing, Frank had just enough time to give me a pleading look before a pack of EMTs surrounded him and essentially shoved me out of the way. I stood up and looked over at the Old Girl, who made brief eye contact with me before returning her gaze to where she would have been able to see Frank had Frank not been encircled by the herd. One of them turned to me and shouted out, "Relative?"

I shook my head no and said, "Passer-by."

Frank rose up from the horde on a mobile stretcher that was being hoisted by a number of emergency workers, his face looking wretchedly confused and sad. I instinctively took a step toward him but was met with the outstretched stiff arms of men decades younger than me, reminding me that I must return to the protocols of distance.

In a quick flurry, Frank was loaded and locked into the back of an ambulance and was gone.

The Old Girl rose from her post at the curb.

The original group of us, minus Frank, remained.

None of us had any idea how to behave in this wholly unprecedented situation. The young man was the first to move. He slowly put his phone into his back pocket and nodded at me and the remaining woman. "Um, bye. I guess," he said. He kicked at something in the street, offered one more slight nod, and walked away.

The woman also put away her phone. "Nice dog," she said.

"Thank you."

"Well, that was something," she said.

"Yes, it was. Something."

"I suppose he'll be all right," she said.

"I think so."

"Frank," she said.

"Yes, Frank. I think he'll be all right."

"Well. All right then," she said. "That's a really nice dog."

"She's a sweetheart," I said, and realized that the young woman might well stand there forever, caught in a whirl of post-traumatic small talk, if I didn't make the first move. "I'd better finish up her walk," I said. And being without a single idea about what I might add, I held up my hand in a friendly wave and began to move away from the scene.

I had the eerie feeling that the site itself was watching the Old Girl and me depart, mourning the conclusion of an episode in time, all remnants of which would soon be gone. If we came back tomorrow, would the Old Girl be able to smell the remains of our pain, our awkwardness, our muddled efforts to be human in such a time as this one?

CHAPTER 39

THE WAY THE MORNING SUN CREATES AN EVER-SHIFTING mosaic of brilliant glints that dance across the surface of the harbor remains as breathtaking as ever. And yet, mornings are entirely changed. What used to be a steady rumble of white noise that the lakefront traffic produced has died down to a murmur, the low purr of a gentle breeze. When the traffic is particularly sparse, I concentrate on individual car engines. I try to identify the make and model by its idiosyncratic sound, but I am still a rank amateur. I can single out V-8 Mustangs, Subaru WRX's and any old VW with an air-cooled engine. That's all so far, but there is time. There is plenty of time.

When we take our morning walk, the Old Girl and I, we make sure to keep the proper distance from the scant number of people we pass. A few still make eye contact, but most do not. It has become too painful. We are dangerous to one another. Most people look straight ahead, as if they are keeping a watch on something in the far distance. I glance sideways as each person approaches, checking to see if they may look toward me. I am prepared to say hello if we both acknowledge our mutual presence, but I am also ready to pass by.

Each day, I look for Cesar. When the Old Girl and I are

nearly home from our morning walk, I look for him. I have been here for less than three months, here in my aerie, my home in the sky, where Cesar was the doorman.

We had already developed a routine, Cesar and I.

Living in a high rise presents drawbacks that must be abided: soulless, blank hallways and metal fire doors and elevators and entire rooms full of institutional mailboxes. In exchange, there is the view, the expanse of water that reaches all the way to its meeting place with the sky. There is a doorman named Cesar, a gentle, ever professional, capable man with a secret sense of irony, a gleam in his eye.

I look across the sidewalk where the dog and I pause, across the wide, blandly landscaped plot of land in front of my building and through the immense picture windows that comprise the front wall of the lobby. In the time before, Cesar knew my schedule. At a certain point in his morning, Cesar would rise from his chair and stand behind the long, glistening wooden desk that marked his domain, and he would wait. When the Old Girl and I reached a certain point, when I looked over, Cesar would give me a full-arm, back-and-forth, get-your-attention-at-any-distance wave. He would keep an utterly straight face. Then, he would sit back down in his chair and resume the work of ensuring that a building with a few hundred individual homes continued to hum along.

Cesar's chair has been empty for more than a week. Not empty, actually, just empty of Cesar. A woman now sits there. A woman who is short enough that all I can see is an impressive crown of hair that appears above the top of the desk, the color of which is difficult to describe. It is not a natural color.

Cesar is not a person who would ever color his hair.

I watch for him.

I hope for him.

Cesar has the Sickness.

It is the day after Frank. It is one day, and it is a lifetime ago. It is the first walk the Old Girl and I have taken since then. It is the thousandth walk we've taken since then. Time has lost all meaning. I think perhaps it was just yesterday that Cesar waved to me, and so the Old Girl and I stop at the precise place on the sidewalk where Cesar is best able to see me. I chance a look. There is nothing but the brassy orange helmet of hair.

A feeling begins in my stomach and inches its way up my throat. I am not sure which I may do first: fall to my knees and vomit onto the sidewalk or witness my own eyes and ears burst from the rage, the rage that this got so fucked up, it got so fucked up, it got *SO FUCKED UP.*

Just a few short weeks ago, on New Year's Eve of 2019, I popped a bottle of really excellent champagne into the refrigerator, and I steeled myself for a few more hours of chipping away at the ceaseless sorting, arranging, and organizing that comprised the last few days leading up to my move. I was headed to the other side of town, to Gino's place. At about that same time on December 31, but on the other side of the world, Chinese Health officials informed the World Health Organization about a cluster of forty-some patients who exhibited a mysterious pneumonia. Most of them could easily be connected to the same place, the Huanan Seafood Market in the city of Wuhan. Chinese authorities closed down the market the following day—New Year's Day of 2020. Just six days later, Chinese officials identified the virus that had caused the pneumonia-like illness. It was a new type of coronavirus which they called nCoV. Four days later, on January 11, the nCoV claimed its first human life. On January 30, less than a full month after the original cluster had been brought to their attention, the World Health Organization declared a "public health emergency of international concern."

He knew.

He was told, more than once he was told, and he knew.

And I thought just then, even more than I had thought every single day for the past four years since he was elected, when I wandered around in a sad confused daze for the entire next day, after he was elected, and I kept wandering up to strangers and saying "How are you doing? How are you doing?" People so scared, so many people telling me how scared they were, how scared to be in this world in this country in this place where they no longer mattered and were no longer safe, not safe in any way, in the country of their birth, not safe. And then the proof, the sickening shocking confirmation behind his lies his inaction his lies his lies and the ugly truth sputtered by that lunatic Texan that if people had to die, if lives had to be lost in the tens, the hundreds, the thousands, the hundreds of thousands, the millions, to keep the machine running, the wheels greased, the engine humming, well, that was an acceptable price to pay, acceptable! There were things that were more important than living, the Texan said. And I thought of it, I thought of the very thing I had been writing about, I thought about my year at the Dreaded School and why I had hated it, I hated it, and fucking Montgomery fucking Treadwell the fucking Third, the warning signal, the harbinger, the one who said it right out loud at the age of eighteen years old, "We're not here to change the world. *We're here to make sure it stays the same.*" That the truly, grotesquely, gargantuanly wealthy and powerful *stay that way.* They keep what they have. They keep it and protect it and make more of it and pass it on to the progeny who will do the same. The rest of us can have our lives where we have to "discover the compensations and refuges for ourselves," like Fitzgerald said, where we struggle and strive and succeed and fail and fail and hope to have the courage, to keep enough courage, please let us please keep enough courage, to get up again when we fall.

Of all the people I met and passed time with at the Dreaded School, it was Rob that I ran into many years later. Rob who hated my coat. Rob whom I wanted to protect. One of those random encounters that happen in our lives against all logic and probability. He shuffled his feet. He ran his fingers through his still-thick hair in the same way I remembered. "Funny, huh?" Rob said. "Tom spent all that time studying Third World countries and going to Third World counties and trying to figure out how to help Third World countries. And now he's in finance. He spends all his time fucking Third World countries."

What happened to us?

I get it now. I get that Montgomery Treadwell III—and the scores of others like him—had always been and would always be the same. But what about Tom? What about the smart, seething boy who had bought me turtlenecks and brought me coffee and handed out flyers side-by-side with me—how did the Toms of the world go from wanting to make real and good and lasting changes to turning tail, wandering away, at the very least looking in the other direction. Or perhaps, as Rob said, *taking part* in fucking over so many others, directly taking part, choking the life out of them with their own bare hands.

What *happened* to us?

The mail comes early to the glass and steel castle. Distressingly early. It is not uncommon for me to return from my morning walk with the Old Girl and find the postal truck taking up a great deal of space in the loading zone, but on this particular day, this day when I am overflowing with despair and anguish and a sorrow so deep, so deep....

The unwieldy boxy bulk of the mail truck enrages me. The mail carrier is in the process of wrestling cartsful of assorted mail through the lobby and into the mailroom. It's a different person than I've seen before, and this enrages me as well, what this says about a world where postal routes are determined by computer mapping, a world where we can't even relish a degree of comfort from seeing a familiar person who brings our mail each day. We are data. We are statistics. We are useful only insofar as we can be manipulated to acquire, obtain, secure, influence, vote, owe, lease, rent, borrow, and buy and buy and buy.

Tussling with the carts of mail requires scant time, I know from past experience, compared to the task of placing the day's delivery into two hundred fifty-two separate locked boxes—which must be unlocked, filled with mail, and locked again. The Old Girl has learned that when she sees the mail carrier busily clanking away in the dismal and featureless mailroom, it is a wise idea to lie down immediately, in case I decide to wait for the person to finish so I might check our mailbox. It's not so much a question of any lofty expectation I may have about a thrilling piece of mail so much as a testimony to my potent disinclination toward an additional elevator ride to check the mail later on. I toss today's options in my head: sit enraged now while I wait an ungodly long time for the mail or be enraged by the elevator later on.

Clinging to the barest modicum of hope that perhaps I will feel less desolate as the day advances—unless I have to face the elevator—I decide to wait.

C H A P T E R 4 0

Dear Esmé,

Back when we were at school, I did not think it was possible to
surprise you, let alone startle you. But startle you I did, when
I spanned the distance of some forty-two years and showed
up at your reading last October. I had come to tell you something important to me. Of course, I had underestimated the
demands there would be on your attention that night, and
there was no opportunity to do much more than surprise you,
quickly tell you that you had made a lasting impact on me,
and offer a heartfelt hug.

I had long thought, Esmé, that there were three women
who were essential to the life that I now have: my mother, for
giving me life, my beautiful wife who has helped shape the
existence that I have and treasure, and you, who saved me
from myself by speaking truth to me when no one else would.
I believe that you changed the course of my life.

It all began our first week at college. You were walking across
the campus, and someone (most likely me) made an inappro-

priate comment. And thank God for it. Nowadays that would probably lead to an uproar, charges, and campus demonstrations, but you had the kindness and spirit that made you want to walk over and talk to the Neanderthal that had dared to speak so. You entered my life that evening, and during that one year you taught me so much—you were a fresh breath of Bohemian air in that pre-Law, pre-Med, pre-Powermonger world. But the moment that really made a difference happened in April. I was spiraling out of control, partying hard every night to forget the fact that I had an impossible amount of work to do. You sought me out, you sat with me, and you reached through the haze with those fateful words: "Tommy, what the fuck are you doing?" From someone else, I would probably have brushed the words off as an annoyance. From you, I took it as a sign of how low I had fallen.

Your words got through to me. *You* got through to me.

I pulled all-nighters every other night for the rest of the semester and climbed the impossible mountain of work that I had created. If you hadn't taken the time to come after me and let me know that you cared, I would have flunked out. I could easily have been a dropout whose life was in tatters. Instead, I graduated and have enjoyed a peaceful and fruitful life that has culminated in the family you see on the card I've sent.

It brings me joy to finally thank you for your kindness way back in the day. Despite the forty-two years, you remain a star in the panoply of my life. You were there when I needed someone, and I will always remember that.

The entire world has changed since I crashed your reading back in October. I have let time slip by since then, and I did not want to wait another minute to tell you how much your kindness impacted my life. Time is more precious than ever, and kindness especially so.

Tommy

CHAPTER 41

I can't wait to show Tommy's letter to Gino.

But I have forgotten that it's Friday. When I walk into our apartment waving the letter above my head in a rather dramatic fashion, Gino gives me a big wave and says to his sisters, "Esmé just walked in. She's waving hi to everyone and sends her love."

Friday morning is Gino's weekly time to video chat with his four sisters, although the concept of "chat" is slightly ludicrous, as Gino generally says next to nothing while his sisters —all of whom live within less than a mile of one another and exist in a revolving door of extended family—talk, interrupt one another, argue, attack one another, defend one another, and ask Gino questions which they then answer themselves.

But Gino loves it. I like to sit in the room just to watch the expressions on his face, his rapt delight at the immersive experience of his big sisters. At the age of seventy-one, he looks, for all the world, like a little boy. The wonder, and the bewilderment, and the miles-deep comfort show on his face. He's here, the little boy who Gino *was,* swept up in the maelstrom of a large Italian family that enfolded him in loud, messy, unceasing, unquestionable love. Right in front of me, seated in the center of a plain gray couch, staring at the laptop that he uses once a week for the sole purpose of this chat.

I sit on the couch that is perpendicular to Gino so I can continue to watch him. The picture windows are behind him, their cloud-level view, the expanse of water and sky that show no change, no sign whatsoever of a sick world.

I scan Tommy's letter and think about the October evening when he came to my reading, the same evening that Gino had suggested I move in with him.

My reading.

The words "reading" stops in its tracks as the thought is moving through my mind. Reading.

CHAPTER 42

DEAR LORD, HOW LONG HAD IT BEEN SINCE I'D THOUGHT about that other reading? Thirty years?

I supposed I had done quite a good job of trying to forget it. No matter that I did not believe in such things; they could still get a grip on me.

I remembered how Liam and I had burst forth from the tent when the reading concluded. Once we were a respectful distance away, I burst into laughter, but it was a distinctly uncomfortable laughter, with an eerie underbelly. Liam picked me up and swung me around in a circle while he laughed; but he searched my face as well.

"Dear God," I said. "I really hope we don't end up some day with no money and no prospects and down to our last $10 and ruing this day, shaking our fists angrily at the sky, as we huddle around the trash can fire with the rest of our homeless compadres, remembering the time when we went to a summer carnival and you pulled me into an astrology tent for a reading or charting or whatever you call it. *Ten dollars,* Liam!"

Liam put me down and rested his hands on his knees, panting slightly from the effort of twirling me. "Worth twice as much. Easily. We will remember this monumental event for the rest of our lives."

"Seriously, who was she talking about? Not me, that's for damn sure!" As I have said before: It is amazing the lies we can tell ourselves.

"It is possible that I beg to differ," he said. "I believe she said that you can be quite timid when it comes to taking real risks, and here you are, proving her right by worrying about my risky, spendthrift ways."

Liam threw both of his arms around me and pulled me in so close that I wasn't sure if our bodies remained entirely separate. He kissed me. Or maybe I kissed him. I often thought that our kisses were more naked than our sex. With the sweet sick smell of cotton candy, and a rickety Ferris wheel churning behind us, and tinny calliope music filling the air, we lost ourselves in a kiss.

Of course, I would remember that night for the rest of my life, deeply buried though it may have been.

Liam was absolutely right.

Liam wore the loose brown shirt that I had found for him, and I wore the long, flowy dress that he had bought for me. I loved the way he looked in that shirt, the way its color made the dark brown of his hair and eyes gleam.

It was 1980, and we were young and broke and always searching for fun, free things to do. Anywhere, really, where we could be together and go about the business of watching the whole spectrum of people living their lives. Food for our thoughts, fuel for our talk, fodder for our writing. How else would I ever have made the acquaintance of Ralph the Swimming Swine, The Watermelon Thump Contest, and Matchstick Marvels Fest. That particular night, Liam and I were strolling hand in hand through a local church's summer carnival. The fair was cheek by jowl with families who seemed to be having an inordinately difficult time keeping track of their children but were bubbling with good spirits nonetheless. Liam and I had just been discussing whether it was unwise to load up on the nearest greasy, fried carnival delight before we tempted fate on the wobbly Ferris wheel and other spinning rides. We decided we could not wait a minute longer for some deliciously trashy food. I thought we were making a beeline for the corn dogs and funnel cakes when Liam tightened his grip on my hand and pulled me toward a quaintly dilapidated tent with a hand painted sign that read "Madame Irene—Readings."

I regretted that we were already inside before I had a chance to quip, "Baby, I don't think it means she's reading Shakespeare."

The summer air inside the tent was thick and still and stifling. Liam and I were dressed for the cool of the evening, and I thought I may well implode from the pressing heat of the air. A woman of indecipherable age sat alone in the tent, her hands folded atop a small round table that had been placed in the center. The woman—Madame Irene, I supposed —had a fountain of jet-black curls and white-pale skin, both of which were set off vividly by dark red lipstick and a similarly colored hairband that wound around her hairline. The hairband had been knotted under one of her ears, and the two long tails draped across her shoulder and reached nearly to her waist. She wore poufy, silky, multi-colored stereotypical gypsy dress. Or blouse, at least, as the table concealed her body below her waist. Her dark eyes had been outlined in thick black liner that made them appear gigantic and hypnotic. The overall impression was breathtaking and comical and commanding all at once.

One empty chair sat opposite her. Though we were in a university town in Iowa, when the woman spoke, her voice revealed a thick Brooklyn accent. My lone year at the Dreaded School had left me with a keen ability to decipher New England accents, including each distinct region of New York City and its environs. Madame Irene looked at Liam and said, "You will have to leave. Or else stand." She looked at me then and said, "As this reading is clearly about *you*. Please, sit."

I took a seat in the empty chair with the dutiful alacrity of a well-trained dog. Liam hesitated, then turned slightly as if he might leave. It was my turn to grasp his hand firmly and say, "No, no. Stay. I want you to stay. We should both hear this." I felt strangely nervous, and I gave him a weak, pleading smile.

Madame Irene took a long look at me, staring fixedly into my eyes while remaining completely silent. At length she said, "I can see it. The major influence in your life is not your sun sign; it's your moon. Not just your moon sign, either, but rather, the phase of the moon on the day that you were born."

I glanced at Liam, and he squeezed my hand. I looked back at the woman. She continued to stare.

"So, unless you happen to know the phase the moon was in, you will need to give me your birthdate."

"Oh," I said. "Of course. I forgot that you're not a psychic." As true now as it was back then, I have always taken refuge in being a wiseass when I'm uneasy.

When I told her the date, she inched her chair back a bit, parted the sumptuous red brocade cloth that draped over the table, and retrieved a stack of ancient looking book pages— Farmer's Almanacs and tide charts going back to 1919, which she consulted for cases like mine, she said, to find the phase of the moon on the day of my birth.

When Madame Irene located the information she sought, she returned the dull brown papers to their hiding place under the table and stared at me for a long time once again.

"You were born under a waxing crescent moon, the very first glimmer of light that the sun casts on the moon the night after the New Moon, when there appears to be no moon in the sky at all. You will be able to find light in the most difficult of circumstances imaginable; this light will never yield for you. This is your great gift.

"Also, you possess a capacity for real joy, a spirit of adventure, and an abiding curiosity. These qualities, combined with your strength and your perseverance will yield a remarkable productivity in your life.

"There are dangers for you, however. Possibly grave dangers. You can be quite timid about taking risks, and this has the potential to hold you back." She cast a glance at Liam before continuing. "You hold on to the past. Too much at times, and this prevents you from living your own life. There will come a time when you will need to wrestle with the ghosts of your past. You will need to face your fears and take a leap of faith —a risk—that you will believe is too difficult, too unmanageable. You must put the past behind you, find faith, take the risk."

Her brow furrowed as she gazed at me silently. "That is what I have to tell you. Let go of ghosts. Take the risk." She folded her hands on the table and gazed straight ahead.

"Thank you," I said. "Have a good evening." I stood, not daring to make eye contact with her, nor Liam either, until he and I were safely outside

She called after me, "Please. Remember my words."

CHAPTER 43

LIAM AND I HAD PLENTY OF TIME FOR THE STRANGE INCIDENT with Madame Irene to fade before we finally got to the end of the long line for funnel cakes. Ravenous hunger overtook our attention as we watched scores of others come away with plates so overladen that the dough spilled well over the sides, so greasy that the useless paper plate was thoroughly soaked with oil in a matter of seconds. I secretly hoped that it wasn't lard, because I intended to live a long life, then reversed my position and secretly hoped that it *was* lard, because you only live once.

"You have to give her credit, really—Madame Irene, that is—for doing a bang-up job of predicting the *past*," Liam said, his funnel cake halfway to his mouth. "I swear that she and I had no prior contact, however eerily her oration gave an astonishing summary of your *recent* life."

"Eerie is right, but I'm not sure about the usefulness of predicting the past. It was a good recap, though. Amazing, really. Heartfelt delivery. No question about that. When she crinkled up her brow and looked a bit alarmed at the end—I was moved. That was a very nice touch."

"Hmmm," Liam said while wrestling a runaway tendril of funnel cake into his mouth.

"I wonder if she travels around with—I don't know—whatever carnival group ferries all those rides from place to place. Or if the church found her. Either possibility seems kind of preposterous. A Brooklyn-born itinerant astrologist versus a transplanted New Yorker now living in the Corn Belt and ferreting out a living. Or trying to ferret out a living. Seems like a tough sell here in Iowa."

"As opposed to the booming business of being a carny?" Liam pointed out.

As Liam and I feasted and rode and strolled, the evening took on the semblance of a dream. Everything seemed to swell at intervals—the noise of the crowd grew louder and higher in pitch, the jangling melodies from competing rides shoved and poked at one another with greater force, the combined smells of human sweat and rancid oil and discarded food overpowered my senses—and then everything would ebb, almost as if the night itself were breathing in and out.

The time in the tent with Madame Irene seemed more and more surreal as I thought about her words. It really was as if she had summarized the past twelve months of my life.

I had met Liam the previous summer in Boulder, Colorado —just over a year before the night at the Iowa carnival. I had attended a writing workshop in the early days of the Naropa Institute, and Liam was one of the assorted faculty. The air between us crackled and sizzled from the moment we laid eyes on one another. I found his paint-stained T-shirt pretentious for a poet; he found my Earth shoes ridiculously overdone. We got into a rather heated conversation the first night there about one of Gary Snyder's poems. The second night, we literally tore one another's clothes in a feverish rush to disrobe. By the end of the three-week workshop, we had become inseparable—not in the physical sense, but rather in the sense that we carried each other around in the e e cummings way: "i carry your heart(i carry it in my heart)."

Liam and I knew that when the workshop was over, I would be returning to the farm where I rented a room, outside of Clarion, Pennsylvania. I would resume my life of writing—earning some pocket money with my tutoring and relishing a rural life where I tended chickens, put up jams, and warmed my feet in front of an ancient stone hearth. Most days I stopped in to visit Mom. Even though she had stopped recognizing me a while ago, she seemed buoyed by my presence. At least some days, she did.

Liam had scored a plum position at the Iowa Writer's Workshop as a guest faculty member. He would be moving to Iowa City to get situated in his new life the same day the Naropa workshop ended. He had shipped much of his stuff to Iowa City before coming to Colorado; the rest of his possessions were crammed into every square inch of the ancient station wagon he had driven to Boulder.

His last words to me, before he got into the station wagon to begin his journey to Iowa were, "A bend in the road is not the end of the road... Unless you fail to make the turn." It was a quote by Helen Keller. I had told Liam that I was obsessed with her as a child.

We had no plan.

Until we did.

In the four months following the workshop's end, Liam made one visit to Clarion, and I made one visit to Iowa City. I delighted in my simple life on the farm, but neither Liam nor I could stand being apart. The only option was for me to move.

"Anne," I said. I had been calling her Anne for a while. For a time, whenever I called her "Mom," either the meaning did not register with her, or she would become agitated and confused. She would make motions as if she were swatting flies away from her face. "I've met someone. We want to be together. I'm going to move to Iowa. Iowa City."

"Why that's wonderful, dear. Wonderful news." I had waited for a day when she was relatively cogent, though I knew better than to think that calling me "dear" was any indication that she knew who I was. Early in Mom's swift decline, she had gotten the idea to call everyone "dear," so she would not have to worry whether she had ever seen them before or not.

There was so little of my mother left.

"I won't be able to visit you very often. I'll be too far away."

"I understand, dear. You've found love," my mother said.

"I miss you so much, Mom. Anne. So, so much."

She looked at me blankly as she sat in her chair by the window with her legs crossed at the knee. It had been years since she had crossed her legs at the ankle in the way she always did before—one of the strongest images I had in my store of memories, the scrapbook of the person my mother had been.

I moved in with Liam, and I never left.

CHAPTER 44

THE CHAT BETWEEN GINO AND HIS SISTERS CONTINUED, SO I picked up Tommy's letter from its cradled place on my lap and re-read it. I did not really remember the conversation that Tommy was referring to. No recollection of any words that I said after, "Tommy, what the fuck are you doing?" I did remember that. I remember his face. He was right about "reaching through the haze." In the corner of his dorm room, he looked like some caricature of a young American white guy you might expect to find in an opium den from a past century. Tommy reclined on a bare mattress, the sheets torn off and crumpled up nearby. Leaning on one elbow, propped up by a stack of pillows, staring at nothing from sickly bloodshot eyes, unable to conjure the dimmest remnant of his big old smile.

"Tommy, what the fuck are you doing?" I may not recall what happened after that, but I would never forget that face that was not Tommy's face at all. Not until I said those words, and his eyes locked onto mine, and he let me see. He let me see *him.* He dropped the veil of his insistent hedonism and laid bare the underbelly—his despair and shame, his dread and fear. There is nothing as compelling, as entreating to me, as a person who shows themselves, their utterly naked, completely vulnerable self. I held out my hand to him. Of course, I did.

Gino's laugh is so effortless, so light, I very nearly expect him to sprout feathers and float up from the sofa. It is always like this when he talks with his sisters. Gino, too, is naked and wide open, but it's blossoming from the opposite side of the despondent anguish that caused Tommy to show himself to me. It's coming not from fear, not from shame, but from love.

Gino smiles at me.

And I know.

Right then, I know.

It never occurred to me that Madame Irene could have been talking about anyone other than Liam. Hadn't I *already* done exactly what she was "predicting?" Hadn't I taken a giant leap of faith to be with a man I'd known for a few short months? Hadn't I needed to wrestle with the long-dead ghost of my father and the living ghost of my mother to move a thousand miles to do just that?

But Madame Irene hadn't been talking about Liam at all; she was talking about Gino.

And whereas all of this is, in fact, truth, it is also, of course, a metaphor.

I had never given Gino a chance. I had stubbornly dwelt in my aggressive ambivalence as if it were a treasured security blanket that I could not abandon—necessary for me to remain intact, safe.

"That is what I have to tell you. Let go of ghosts. Take the risk." Madame Irene's words. Dear God, had my life actually come to this? Was I really a late middle-aged writer who believed that her future had been foretold by a New York hustler posing as a mystic astrologer at a church carnival in Iowa?

Well, not exactly. I was a late middle-aged writer who was harkening back to words uttered in a stifling little tent many, many years ago—words that traversed time and whispered in my ear, words that hit the proverbial nail of my current life squarely on the head. In other words, I heeded the metaphor.

Liam and I met at a place and time that was right for us both, and we fell into one another's arms. I shed the armor of the proud and determined loneliness that I had carried since my father died, and I let Liam in. When Liam died, I picked that armor back up, and I darned the chinks and fissures painstakingly, meticulously, until I had made it even stronger than it had been before. No one got in; I made sure of it. Not friends, not lovers. Maybe especially not lovers; how easy it is to slip comfortably into sex—even passionate sex, sensual bestial sex—with no real, human exchange of any substance whatsoever.

Forty-two years ago, I held out my hand to Tommy. He said I made a difference. He said my simple act of caring changed the trajectory of his teetering, spiraling life.

Yesterday I held out my hand to Frank. Despite the dangers and divides of a troubled world, I held it out.

All I did was care for a fellow human being.

When did so many of us stop doing this?

When I sit down to write, when the blank void of an unwritten page faces me, I don't think about the thousands of people who may read my book. I think about one. One person who may close the cover after they have read the last pages, put the book down, and walk away changed. Even in the smallest way: changed.

Beyond Gino, the expanse of water is the steely color that reveals the coming of spring, a rich gray that bears the nascent signs of blue.

Gino is a genuinely good man, a solid man. And God knows, he is a patient man—patient enough to hold fast to the belief, the hope, that I would come around. He has been holding out his hand to me for a long, long time, while I held an unyielding shield.

When Gino finishes his call, I will hold out my hand.

ACKNOWLEDGMENTS

The Reading marks the third book that I have published with Amika Press. I have always been grateful for Amika's dedication and commitment to my books, but I say without reservation that the Amika partners have gone well above and beyond my wildest expectations. What editor enthusiastically agrees to take a look at your *first draft?* John Manos. What book designer/production person offers to be your earliest reader, eagerly snapping up sections of a new book where the proverbial ink is still wet? Sarah Koz. I cannot thank these two folks highly enough.

My confused but dedicated writing group has continued to provide me with invaluable feedback despite my presenting material completely out of sequence with no possible sense of continuity. They are also dear friends whose depth of support remains a foundation for me. Thank you Mirelle Bloch, Bill Horstman, and Brooke Laufer.

Several of the same people have been early readers for me since the beginning of my book writing. They are invaluable, and I wholeheartedly sing the praises of Karen Monier, James R. Petersen and Janis Post.

Philip Roth said that the family of a writer is doomed. I believe my own family would concur, though they will be thrilled to see neither themselves nor anyone that they recognize in *The Reading*. Even while cringing, they celebrate me. It means everything. It is also true that Michelle Cardozo, Taylor Hales, Molly Hales and Jared Slucter are among my favorite people on the entire planet.

A sincere thanks to each person who reads this book and opens themselves up to the possibility of being changed.

Barbara Monier has been writing since her earliest days when she composed in crayon on paper with extremely wide lines. She studied writing at Yale University and the University of Michigan. While at Michigan, she worked independently with poet Robert Hayden. Also at Michigan, she received the Avery and Jule Hopwood Prize. It was the highest prize awarded that year and the first in Michigan's history for a piece written directly for the screen. *The Reading* (2022) is her fifth published novel. *The Rocky Orchard* (2020) was awarded the Silver Medal for Literary Fiction, Readers' Favorite Awards. *Pushing the River* (2018) won the Bronze Award for Literary Fiction, Readers' Favorite Awards.

Made in the USA
Middletown, DE
01 October 2022

11602558R00150